NEWS.
TELEGRAPH

The [masthead partly covered by barcode]

NEWS.
TELEGRAPH

Vol 76 · No 318 NEW YORK, NY MONDAY, NOVEMBER 14 ~ 1904 EVENING EDITION

PTERODACTYL HUNTERS

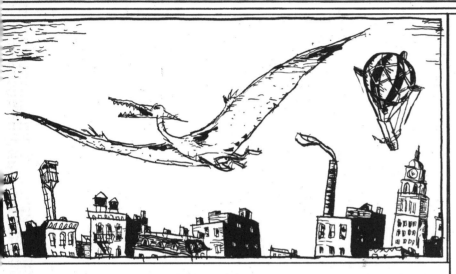

BATTLE ABOVE THE BOWERY

SULLIVAN SLAYS PTERO JUST BEFORE SUNRISE

VOWS TO ELIMINATE BEASTS BY '05

MAYOR McCLELLAN PLEDGES FULL SUPPORT TO PTERO PATROL

PTERODACTYL COMMISSION TO DISPOSE OF CARCASS

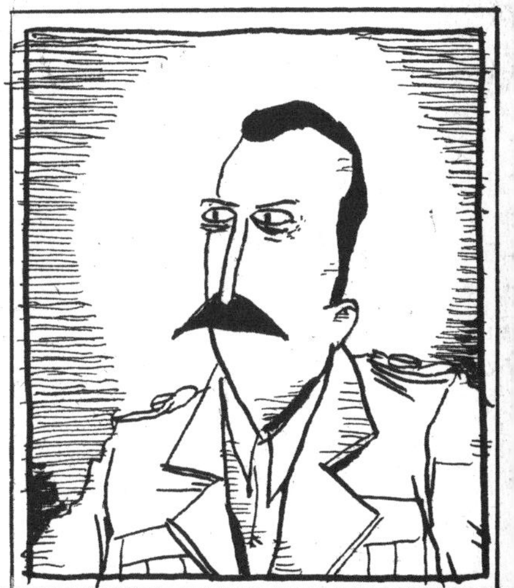

LATE NIGHT HUNT LEADS TO FIRST KILL IN MONTHS

END OF PTERO TERROR?

General Slocum, a three-decked excursion steamer, the largest in these waters, more than six hundred persons, the majority of whom were women and children, were burned to death or drowned by jumping overboard or by being thrown into the whirlpools of Hell Gate in the burning of the vessel.

Approximately five hundred bodies have been recovered and now are being tagged in the morgues of Bellevue Hospital and Harlem. Divers are still busy taking bodies from the hold of the vessel which, it is said, is choked with bodies, and hundreds who leaped or were thrown into the river have not been recovered.

Great preparations had been made for the seventeenth annual excursion to Locust Grove of the Sunday School of St. Mark's German Lutheran Church, the congregation of which Church is drawn from the lower East and West Sides.

More Than 2,000 Aboard.

It is variously estimated that there were between 1,500 and 2,500 persons on board the General Slocum when she left the pier at Third street, East river, through the Knickerbocker Steamboat Company, which owns the General Slocum, officially states that the number of passengers was 8?3. It is thought, however, that there were several hundreds of children in arms.

The scenes on the decks of the steamer as she proceeded up the East river was one of merrymaking. Flags on the vessel fluttered in the June breezes, the bands were playing and the children were singing, dancing or waving handkerchiefs and hats in answer to the salutations of those on shore or from passing steamers.

DO INFREQUENT SIGHTINGS MEAN EXTINCTION IS NEAR?

THE SLOCUM CATASTROPHE RECALLS A LIKE DISASTER

Burning and Beaching of the Seawanhaka in 1880 in a Way Similar to the Latest East River Horror.

SPECIAL TO THE POST-STANDARD.

NEW YORK, June 16.—The burning and beaching of the General Slocum, with the loss of scores of lives, recalls vividly the Seawanhaka disaster, which at the time was considered the worst catastrophe that had happened to a steamboat in this harbor. The vessel was burned and beached in a way similar to the General Slocum, and a great number of lives were lost.

On June 28, 1880, the steamer Seawanhaka, running from Peck Slip to Glen Cove, L. I., with more than 300 passengers on board, was burned off Wards Island at about 5 p. m. The flames, which were preceded by an explosion near the engine room, spread through the vessel with great rapidity, causing a terrible scene of confusion and panic.

Many persons jumped overboard, while women and children were knocked down and trampled on the decks. A number who jumped or were pushed overboard were drowned, while others were picked up by small boats.

Capt. Charles P. Smith headed the boat for the Sunken Meadows, a marshy island a little north of Wards Island and there beached her. There many passengers dropped off into the shallow water, while others had been burned alive on the decks.

The injured were taken for hospital treatment to Wards and Randall's Island.

The list of the dead numbered thirty-two, when made up three days later, and at that time thirty persons were missing, who were believed to have been on the steamer.

Assistant District-Attorney of New York Declares the Catastrophe Will be Sifted to the Bottom.

BY THE ASSOCIATED PRESS.

NEW YORK, June 15.—Assistant District-Attorney Garvin was at the scene of the wreck of the General Slocum today for some hours. He said that he would subpoena the entire crew and as many of the survivors as possible and would make every effort to fix the responsibility for the catastrophe.

Charles E. Hill, a director of the Knickerbocker Steamboat Company, visited the Lebanon Hospital late to-day to see Captain Van Schaick, the commander of the General Slocum, who had been taken there earlier in the day under arrest. After a talk with him Mr. Hill said that the captain did not know the cause of the fire.

"The cause of the fire is not known,"

... reach North Brother Island was Dr. Henry Krauskopf, house surgeon of the Harlem Hospital. "It was the most dreadful spectacle I ever saw," he said. "Lying about in various postures were hundreds, so it seemed, of women and a few children. All seemed to be appealing for help at one time, the most touching appeals being from mothers for their children. There were children all about us lying dead on the grass. In the three hours that we were on the island I think we must have treated fully 150 persons."

Mrs. Martha Weiss says that while she was struggling in the water a boat pulled up alongside of her and she was stripped of her rings, earrings, brooch and then pushed back in the water. She was later rescued in an unconscious condition by another boat and taken to the island.

So far as known to-night only one of

Dead and Injured Numbered Among Members, Relatives and Acquaintances.

When the news of the burning of the General Slocum and the attendant loss of life was received yesterday by the members of the conference of the Evangelical Lutheran Synod, now in session here at Zion Church, a feeling of personal sorrow pervaded the assemblage. The synod includes New York and New Jersey, and to many of the visitors the pastor and members of the ill-fated congregation of St. Mark's were close friends.

Hundreds of residents of the North Side have mourned the loss of friends and acquaintances. Rev. and Mrs. George C. F. Haas are well known here, the latter having been a frequent visitor in past years. Many of the visitors have relatives and

K. CALDWELL ILL TAKES A REST

Postmaster-General Unable to Preside in Chicago.

CONDITION IS NOT SERIOUS

Weakness Will Keep Him from Con-

MINERS DRIVEN TO NEW MEXICO

Soldiers Order Them Not to Return to Colorado.

THEIR CAPTORS ARE JEERED

Deported Workers Sing "Sweet Land of Liberty"—Men Cross the Line and Return to the State.

BY THE ASSOCIATED PRESS.

ANTONITO, Col., June 15.—Thirty-six union miners and sympathizers, deported from the Cripple Creek district, were unloaded from the special train near the New Mexico line to-day and were driven by the guard under command of Lieutenant Colonel ...

PTERODACTYL COMMISSION REMEMBERS FALLEN HUNTERS

IT IS WITH GREAT HUMILITY AND UNENDING THANKS THAT THE CITY OF N. YORK HONORS THE FOLLOWING PATROLMEN:

D. MAZZUCCHELLI	D. SANDLIN
M. ARISMAN	G. PANTER
T. HART	K. MAYERSON
M. NEWGARDEN	A. ROBERTS

BY THE ASSOCIATED PRESS.

NEW YORK, June 15.—Assistant District-Attorney Garvin was at the scene of the wreck of the General Slocum today for some hours. He said that he would subpoena the entire crew and as many of the survivors as possible and

reach North Brother Island was Dr. Henry Krauskopf, house surgeon of the Harlem Hospital. "It was the most dreadful spectacle I ever saw," he said. "Lying about in various postures were hundreds, so it seemed, of women and a few children. All seemed to be appealing for help at one time, the most touching ap-

BROOKLYN MAN'S BODY FOUND IN WOODS:

Pterodactyl historian and former Junior Pterodactyl Patrol PFC, BRENDAN C. LEACH,

Harry L. Preston Believed to Have Swallowed Poison.

ROCHESTER, June 15.—The body of Harry L. Preston was found this morning in an isolated portion of some woods inside the city limits. No marks of a bullet or knife were discernible and it is thought that he committed suicide by poison. Preston was for many years associated with Prof. Henry Ward at the Ward Natural Science Museum. He was despondent over business affairs.

BY THE ASSOCIATED PRESS.

LONDON, June 16—(Thursday).—A dispatch to The Daily Express from Tokio, dated June 15, says news has been received there, but has not yet been officially published, of a great Japanese victory near Fu-chou, on the railway, seventy miles north of Port Arthur.

The Russians, it is added, were overwhelmed, lost 1,600 men, left all their guns on the field and retreated in disorder.

The Daily Chronicle's correspondent at Tokio cables the same news, adding that the Russians to the number of 7,000 men are now in full flight toward Tahi-chaiao and Kaio-chow.

JAPANESE CUT DOWN IN VAFANGOW BATTLE.

Three Squadrons of Cavalry Destroyed by the Russians.

BY THE ASSOCIATED PRESS.

LONDON, June 15.—The correspondent of The Central News at Liao-yang telegraphed to-day as follows:

"The fighting at Vafangow (about sixty-five miles north of Port Arthur) was renewed to-day and is still proceeding. No details are obtainable, but there are persistent rumors that the Russians were partly successful, destroying three squadrons of cavalry and making prisoners of sixty men. The Russian casualties in the fighting yesterday were 3?8 men killed or wounded. The Japanese casualties are not known.

"Later a section of Russian cavalry marching in the direction of Tafan-chow and Lan-kee discovered on its right flank a great force of Japanese cavalry.

"An engagement ensued, and, according to the latest dispatches, fighting is proceeding all along the line, the Japanese having obtained re-enforcements from Vafangow consisting of three infantry divisions with artillery and cavalry."

JAPS MAKE ASSAULT IN TREMENDOUS FORCE

LIAO-YANG, June 16.—The battle of Vafangow lasted till 8 o'clock yesterday evening. The Japanese, in tremendous force, attacked the Russian position but

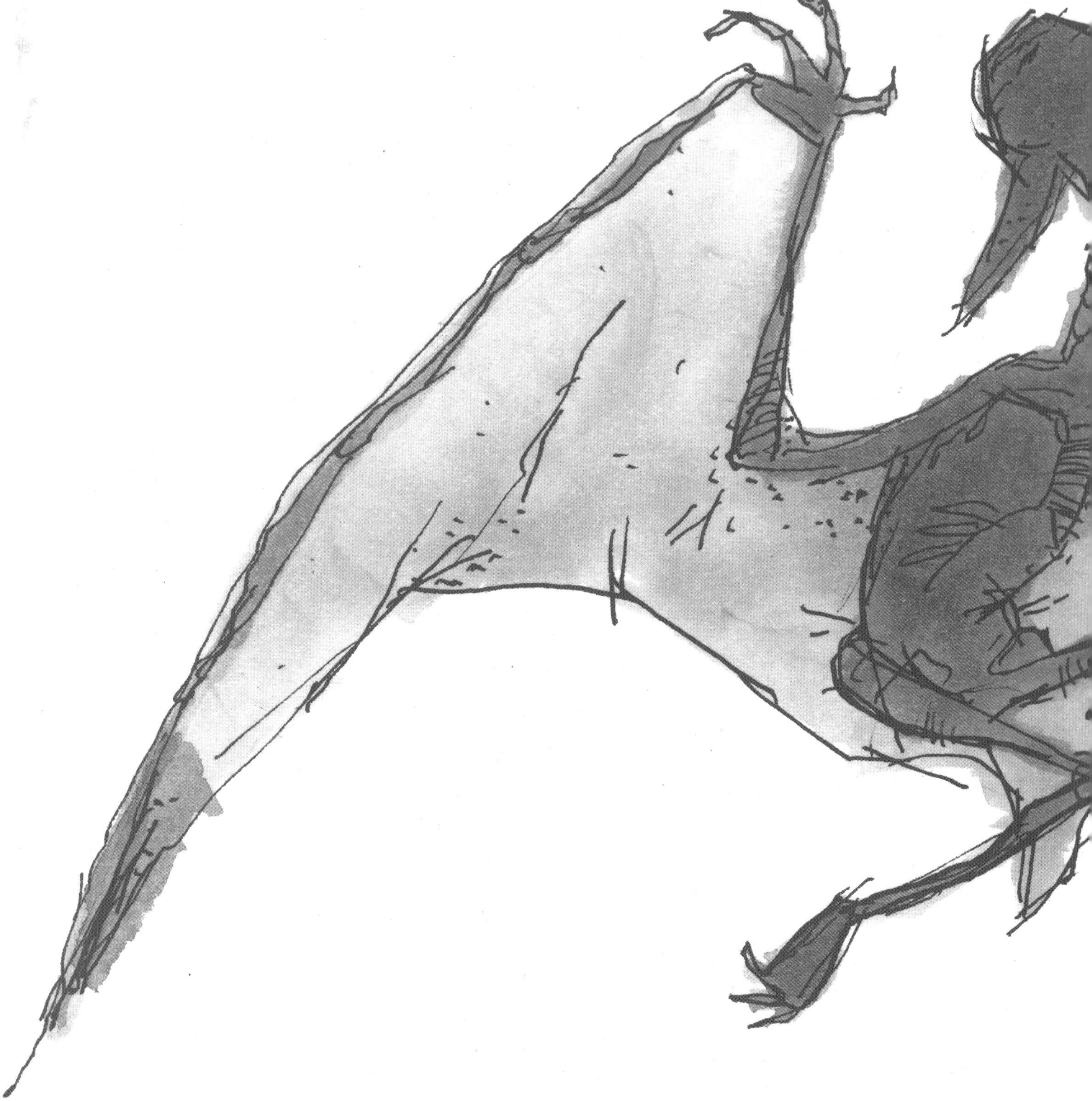

THE PTERODACTYL HUNTERS IN THE GILDED CITY

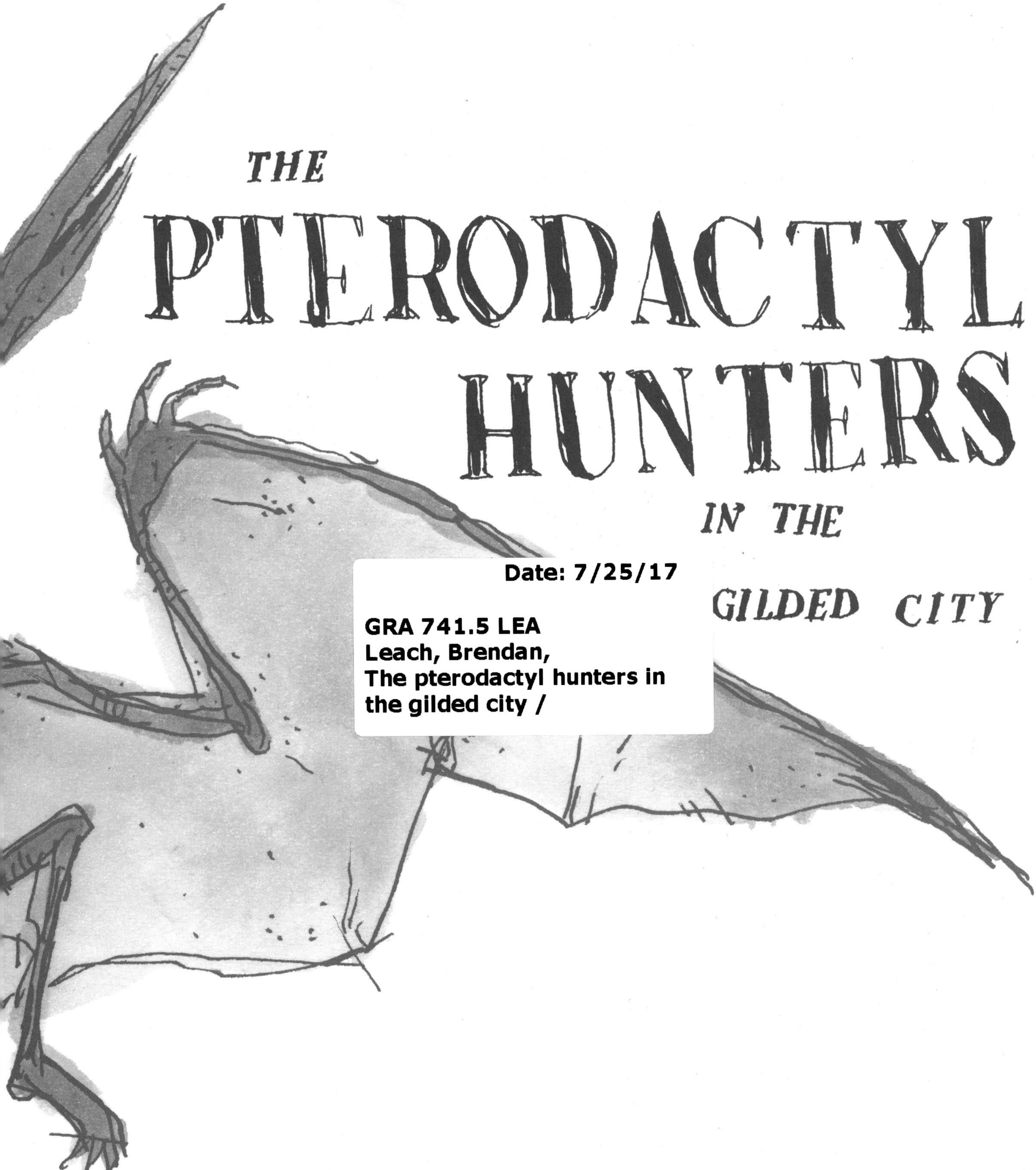

BY BRENDAN LEACH

SPECIAL THANKS TO:

DAVID MAZZUCCHELLI
DAVID SANDLIN
MARSHALL ARISMAN
GARY PANTER
TOM HART
KEITH MAYERSON
LEON AVELINO
BARRY MATTHEWS
CHRIS STAROS
LEIGH WALTON
KRISTY CALDWELL
KEVIN NIBLEY
ROB O'NEILL
BARBARAJEAN MAJEWSKI

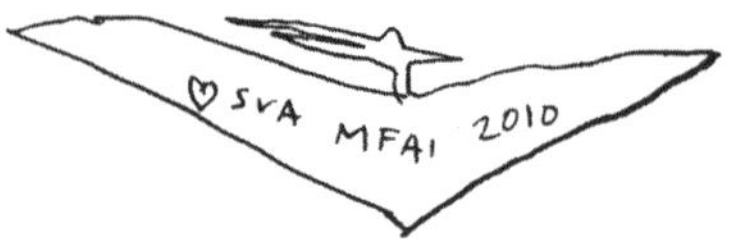
♡ SVA MFA1 2010

THIRD EDITION - SEPTEMBER 2016

PRINTED IN CHINA

ISBN-13: 978-0-9962739-3-0
ISBN-10: 0-9962739-3-X

SAB-032

LIBRARY OF CONGRESS PCN: 2016940313

PUBLISHED BY SECRET ACRES
237 FLATBUSH AVENUE, #331
BROOKLYN, NY 11217

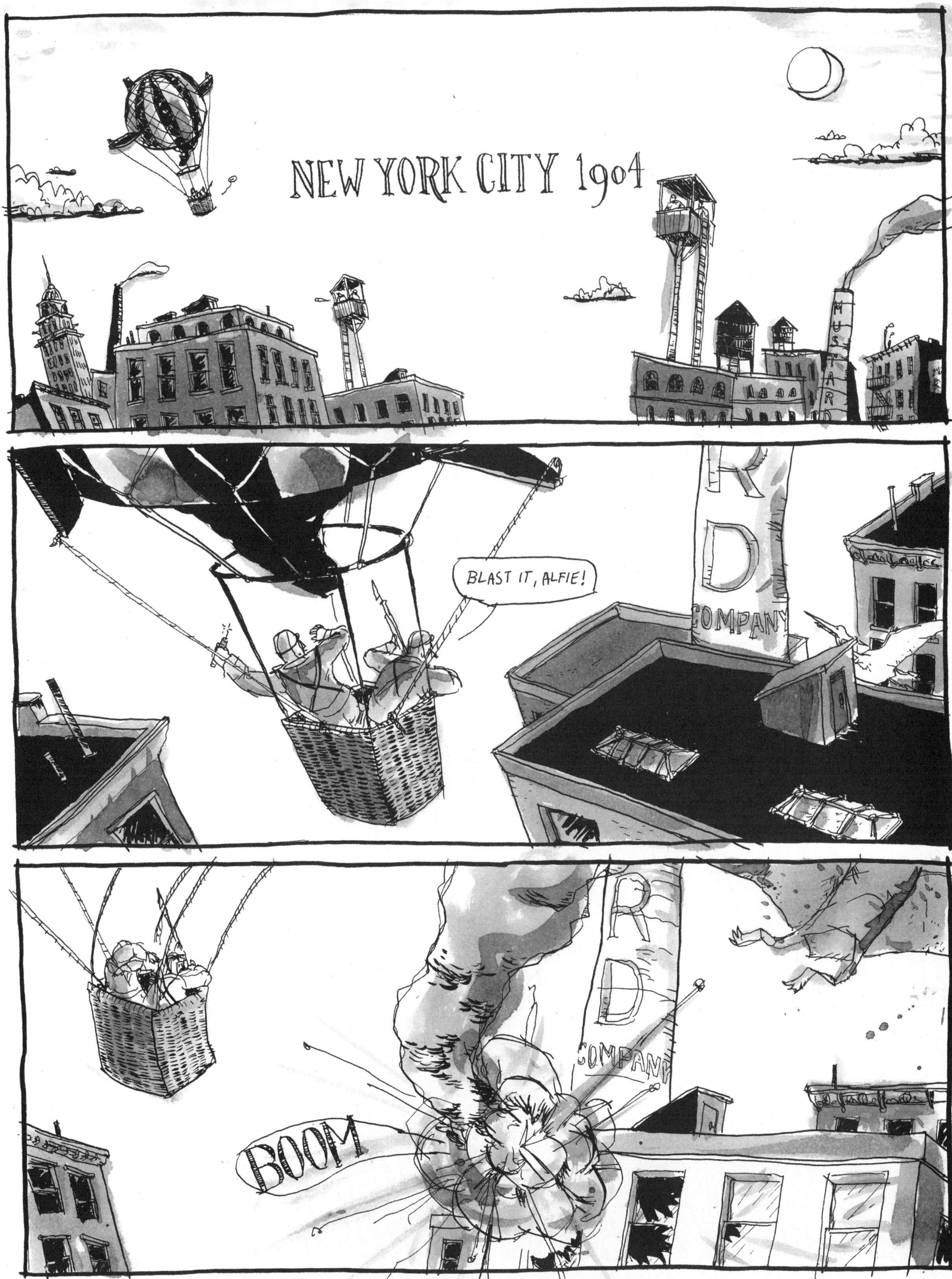
NEW YORK CITY 1904
BLAST IT, ALFIE!
BOOM

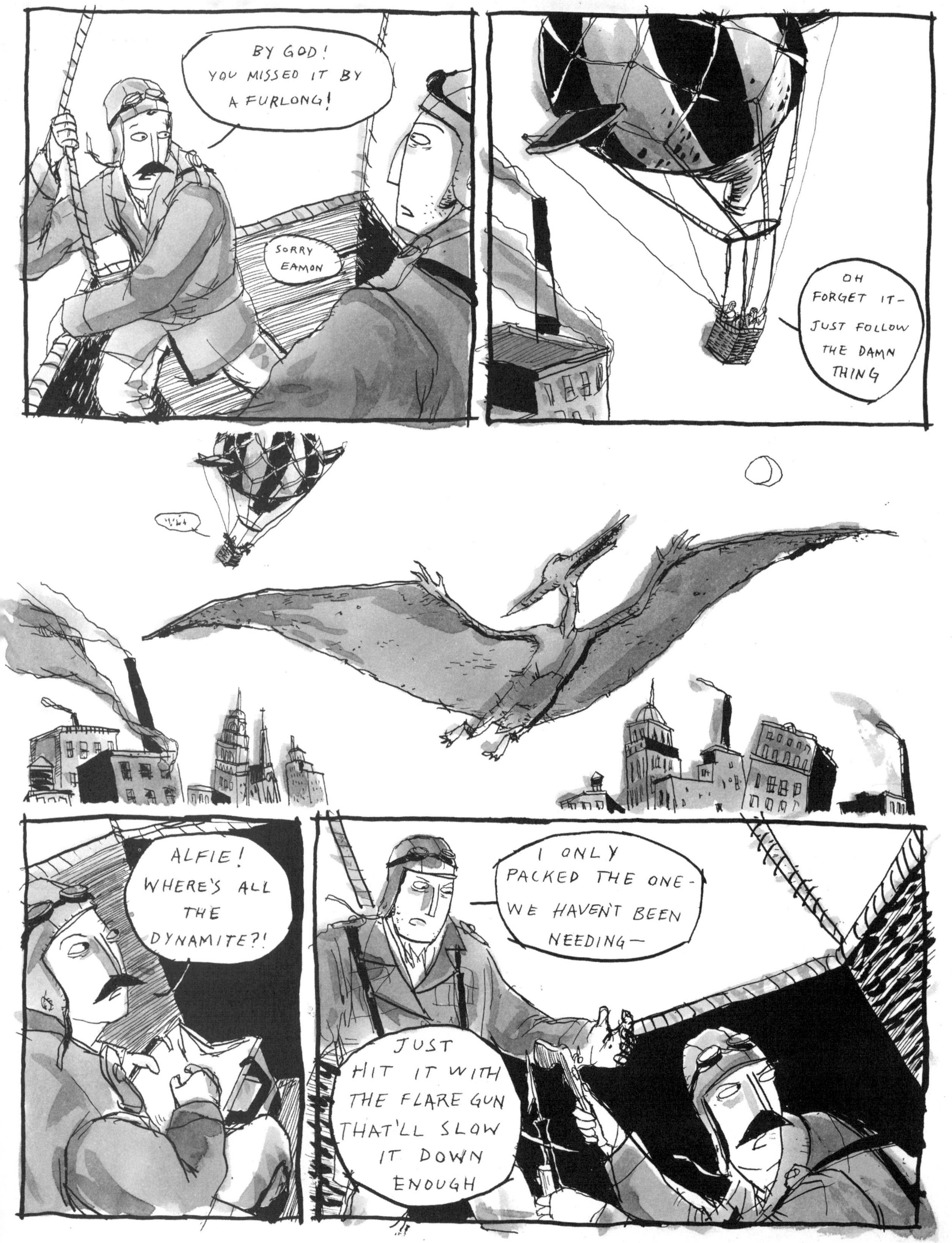
BY GOD! YOU MISSED IT BY A FURLONG!
SORRY EAMON
OH FORGET IT- JUST FOLLOW THE DAMN THING
ALFIE! WHERE'S ALL THE DYNAMITE?!
I ONLY PACKED THE ONE- WE HAVEN'T BEEN NEEDING—
JUST HIT IT WITH THE FLARE GUN THAT'LL SLOW IT DOWN ENOUGH

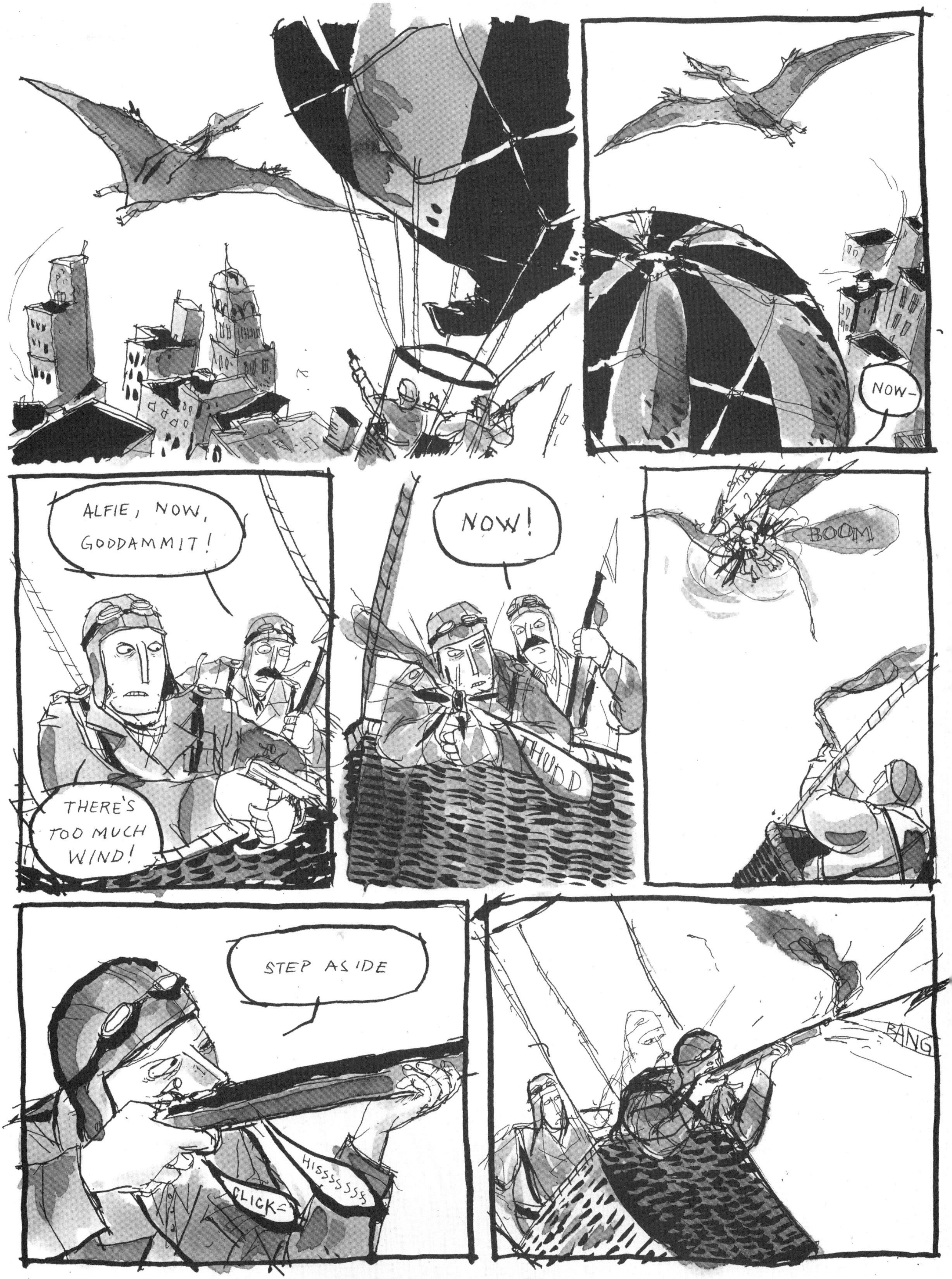
NOW-
ALFIE, NOW, GODDAMMIT!
THERE'S TOO MUCH WIND!
NOW!
THUDD
BOOM
STEP ASIDE
CLICK-
HISSSSSSS
BANG

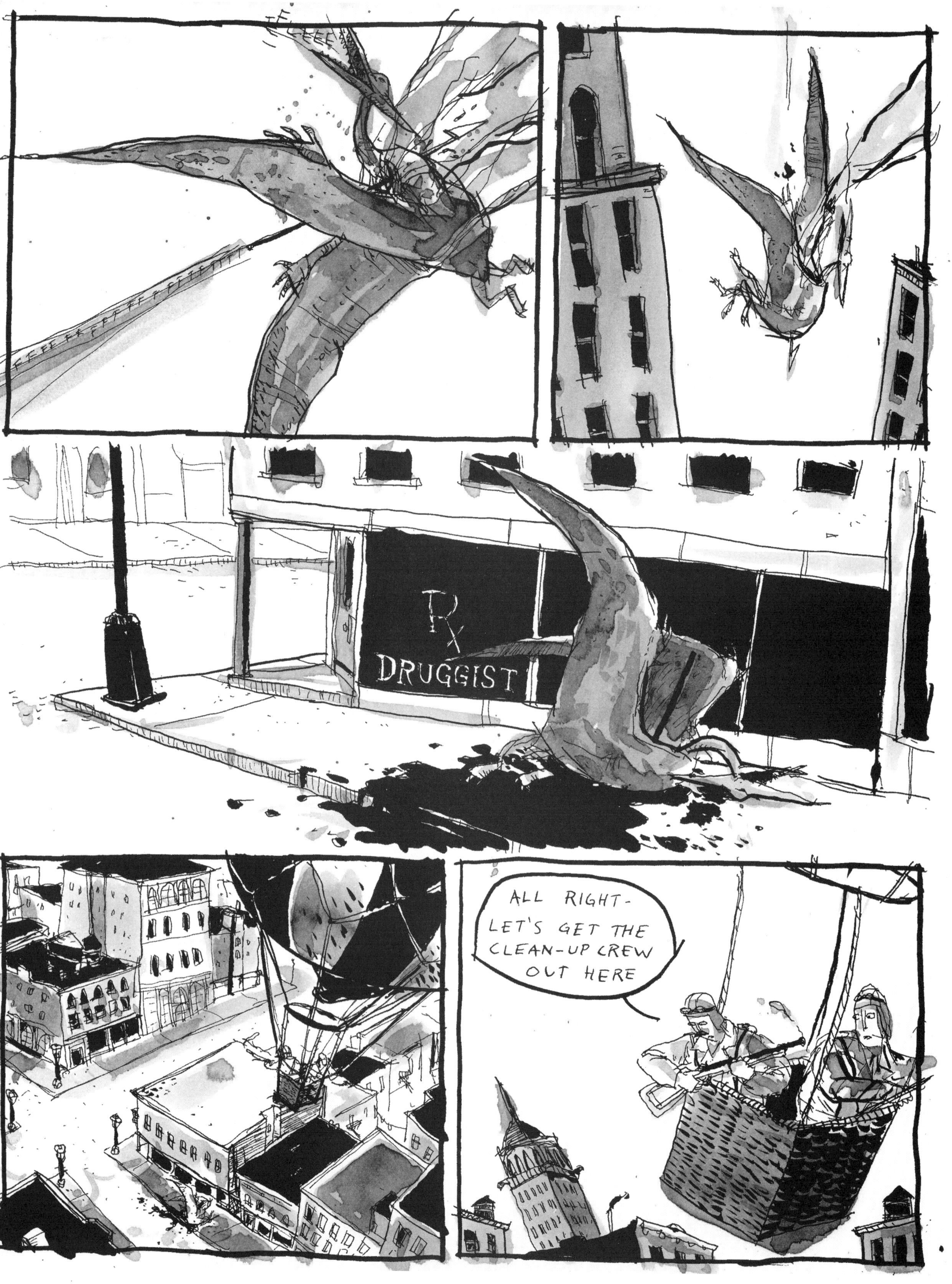
R
DRUGGIST
ALL RIGHT-
LET'S GET THE
CLEAN-UP CREW
OUT HERE

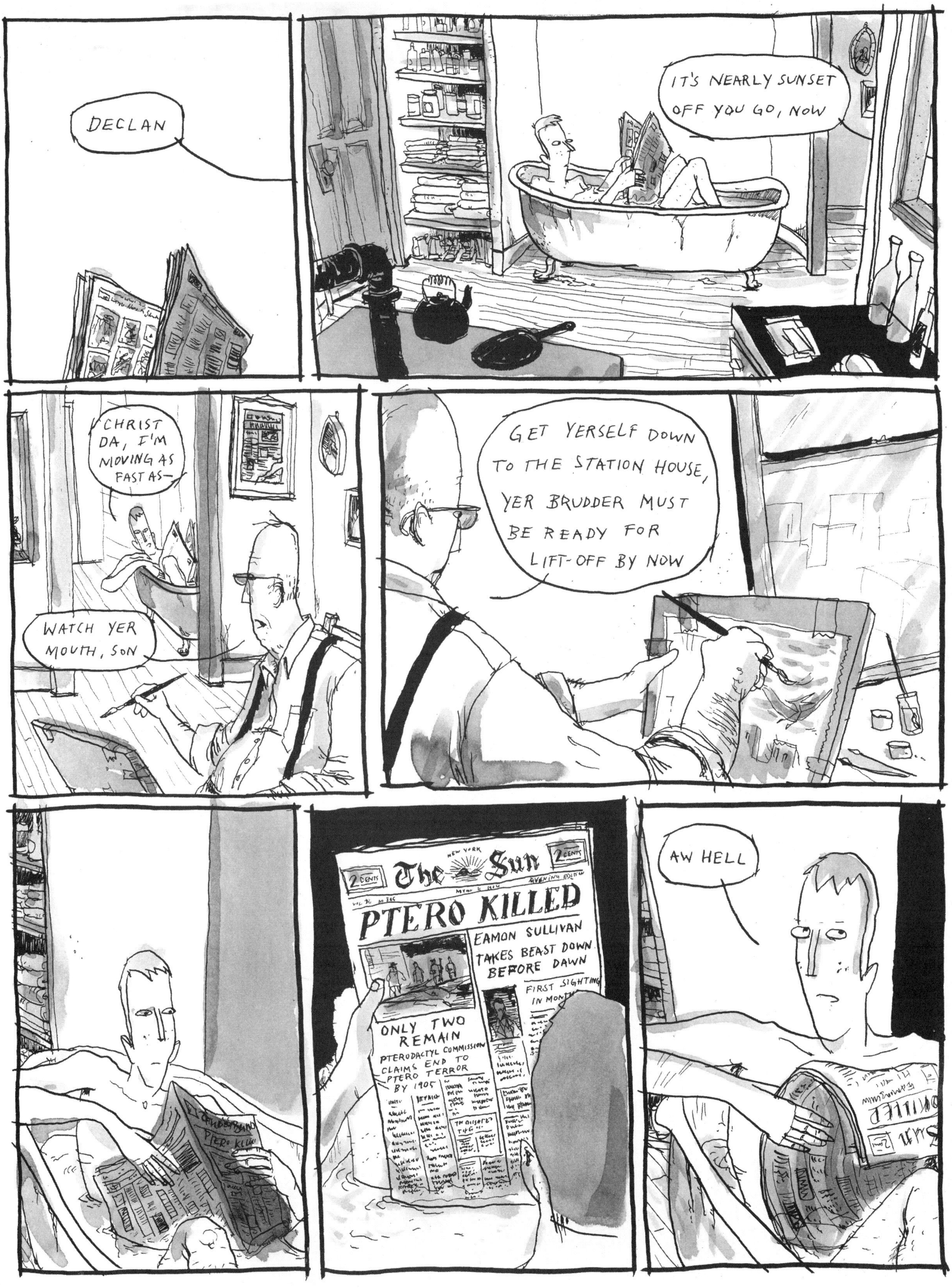
DECLAN
IT'S NEARLY SUNSET OFF YOU GO, NOW
CHRIST DA, I'M MOVING AS FAST AS—
WATCH YER MOUTH, SON
GET YERSELF DOWN TO THE STATION HOUSE, YER BRUDDER MUST BE READY FOR LIFT-OFF BY NOW
NEW YORK
The Sun
2 CENTS
PTERO KILLED
EAMON SULLIVAN
TAKES BEAST DOWN BEFORE DAWN
FIRST SIGHTING
ONLY TWO REMAIN
PTERODACTYL COMMISSION CLAIMS END TO PTERO TERROR BY 1905
AW HELL

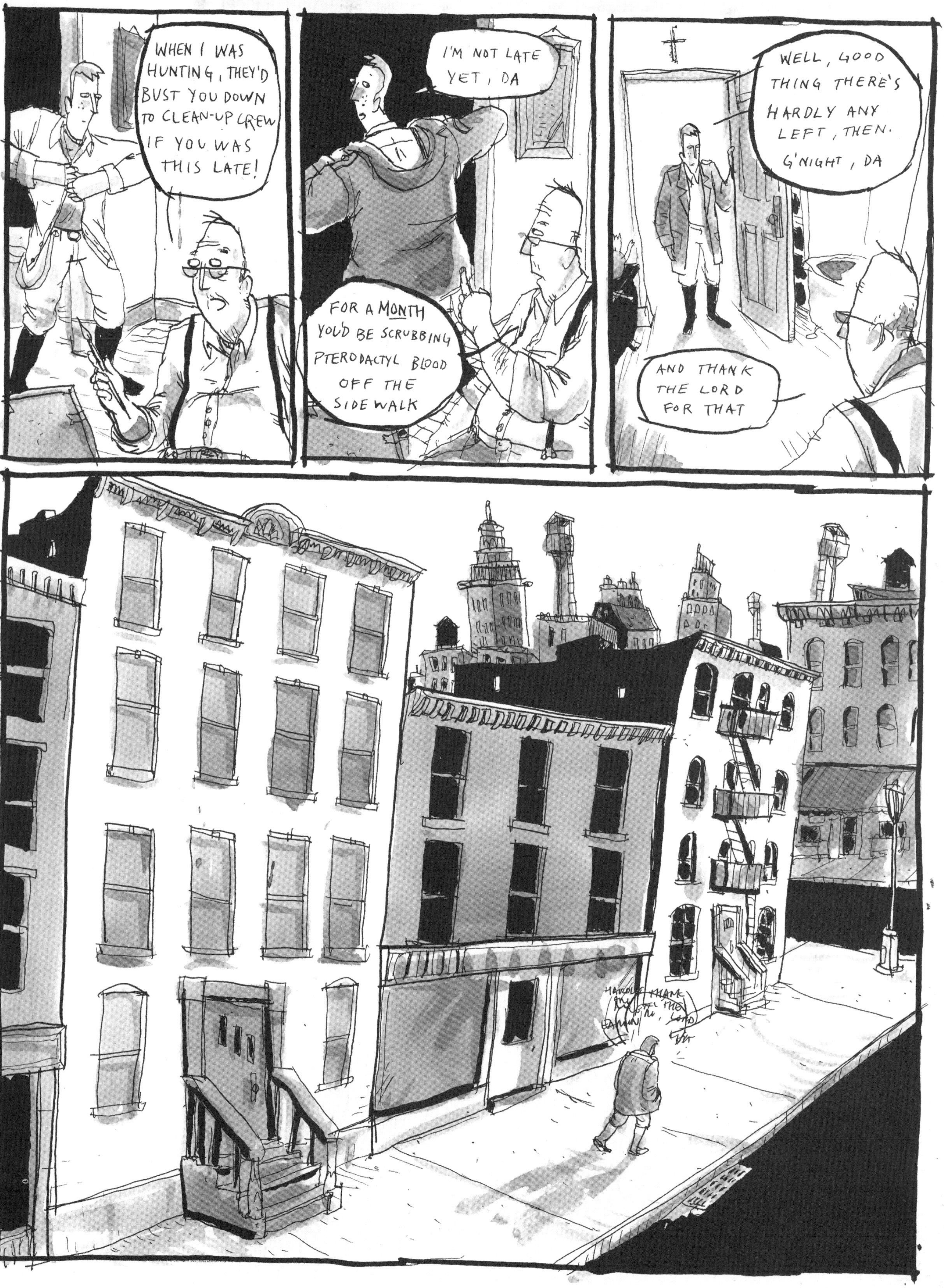
WHEN I WAS HUNTING, THEY'D BUST YOU DOWN TO CLEAN-UP CREW IF YOU WAS THIS LATE!
I'M NOT LATE YET, DA
FOR A MONTH YOU'D BE SCRUBBING PTERODACTYL BLOOD OFF THE SIDEWALK
WELL, GOOD THING THERE'S HARDLY ANY LEFT, THEN. G'NIGHT, DA
AND THANK THE LORD FOR THAT

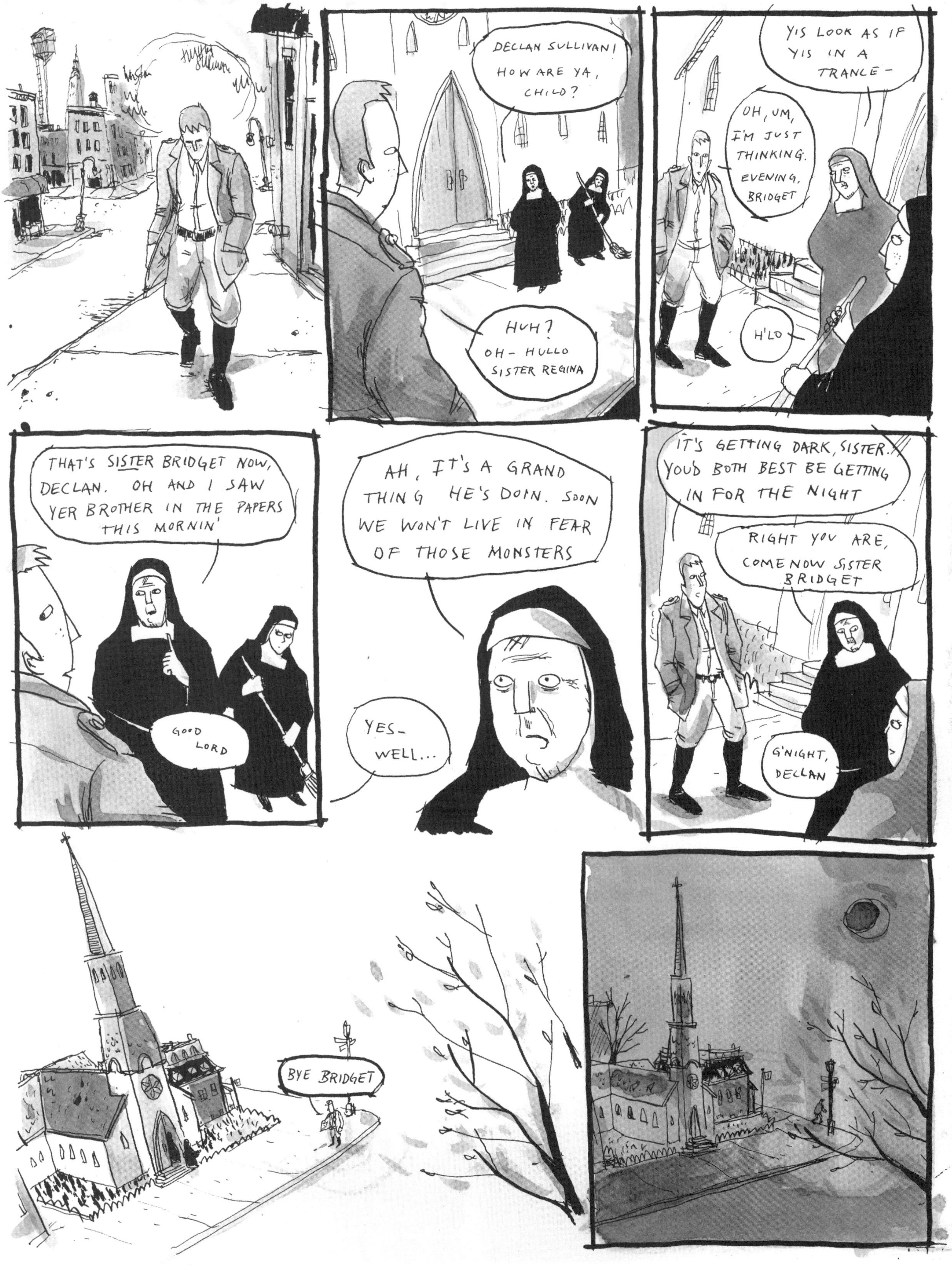
DECLAN SULLIVAN! HOW ARE YA, CHILD?
HUH? OH- HULLO SISTER REGINA
YIS LOOK AS IF YIS IN A TRANCE-
OH, UM, I'M JUST THINKING. EVENING, BRIDGET
H'LO
THAT'S SISTER BRIDGET NOW, DECLAN. OH AND I SAW YER BROTHER IN THE PAPERS THIS MORNIN'
GOOD LORD
AH, IT'S A GRAND THING HE'S DOIN. SOON WE WON'T LIVE IN FEAR OF THOSE MONSTERS
YES- WELL...
IT'S GETTING DARK, SISTER. YOU'D BOTH BEST BE GETTING IN FOR THE NIGHT
RIGHT YOU ARE, COME NOW SISTER BRIDGET
G'NIGHT, DECLAN
BYE BRIDGET

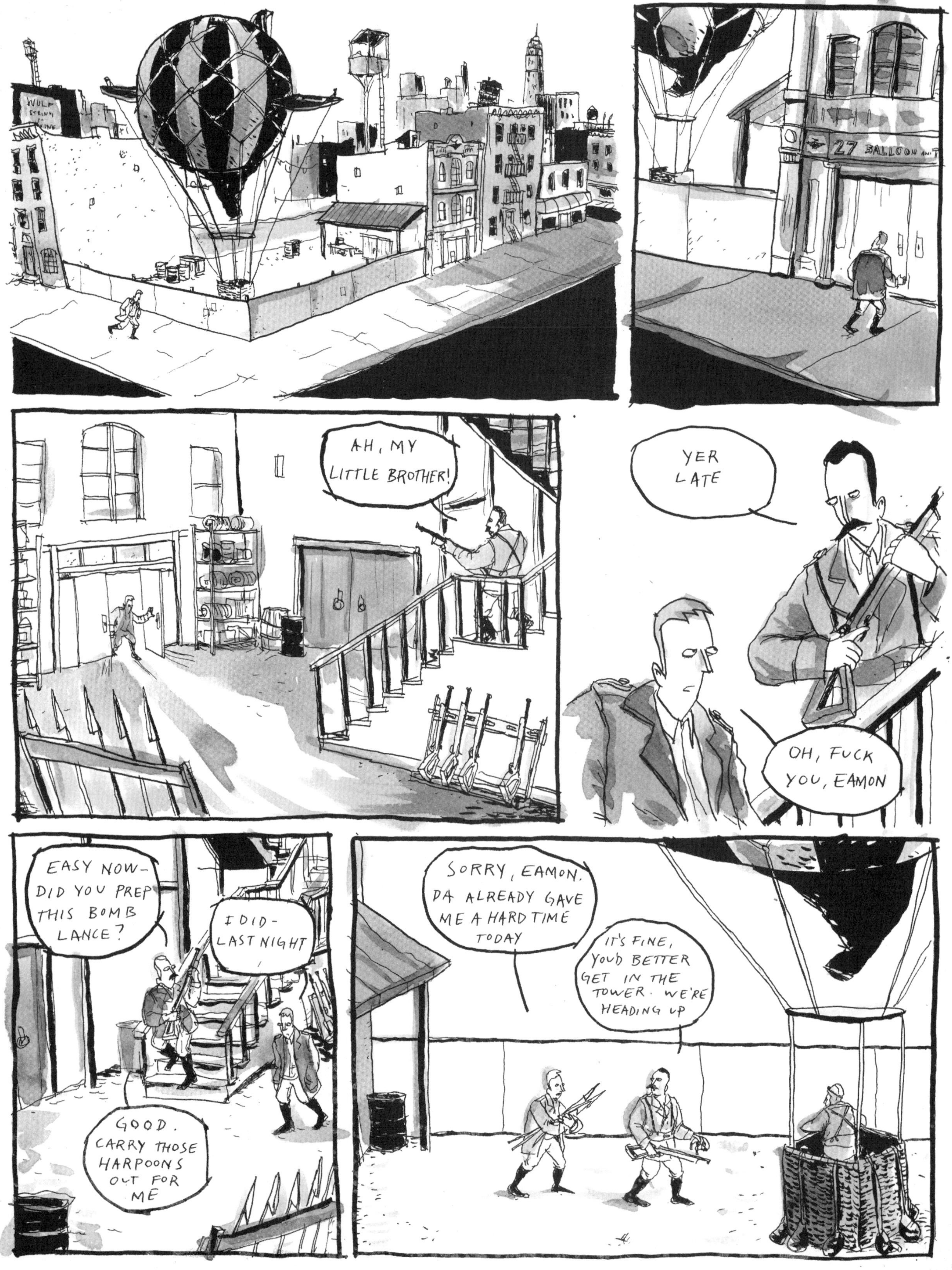
WOLF
27 BALLOON
AH, MY LITTLE BROTHER!
YER LATE
OH, FUCK YOU, EAMON
EASY NOW- DID YOU PREP THIS BOMB LANCE?
I DID- LAST NIGHT
GOOD. CARRY THOSE HARPOONS OUT FOR ME
SORRY, EAMON. DA ALREADY GAVE ME A HARD TIME TODAY
IT'S FINE, YOU'D BETTER GET IN THE TOWER. WE'RE HEADING UP

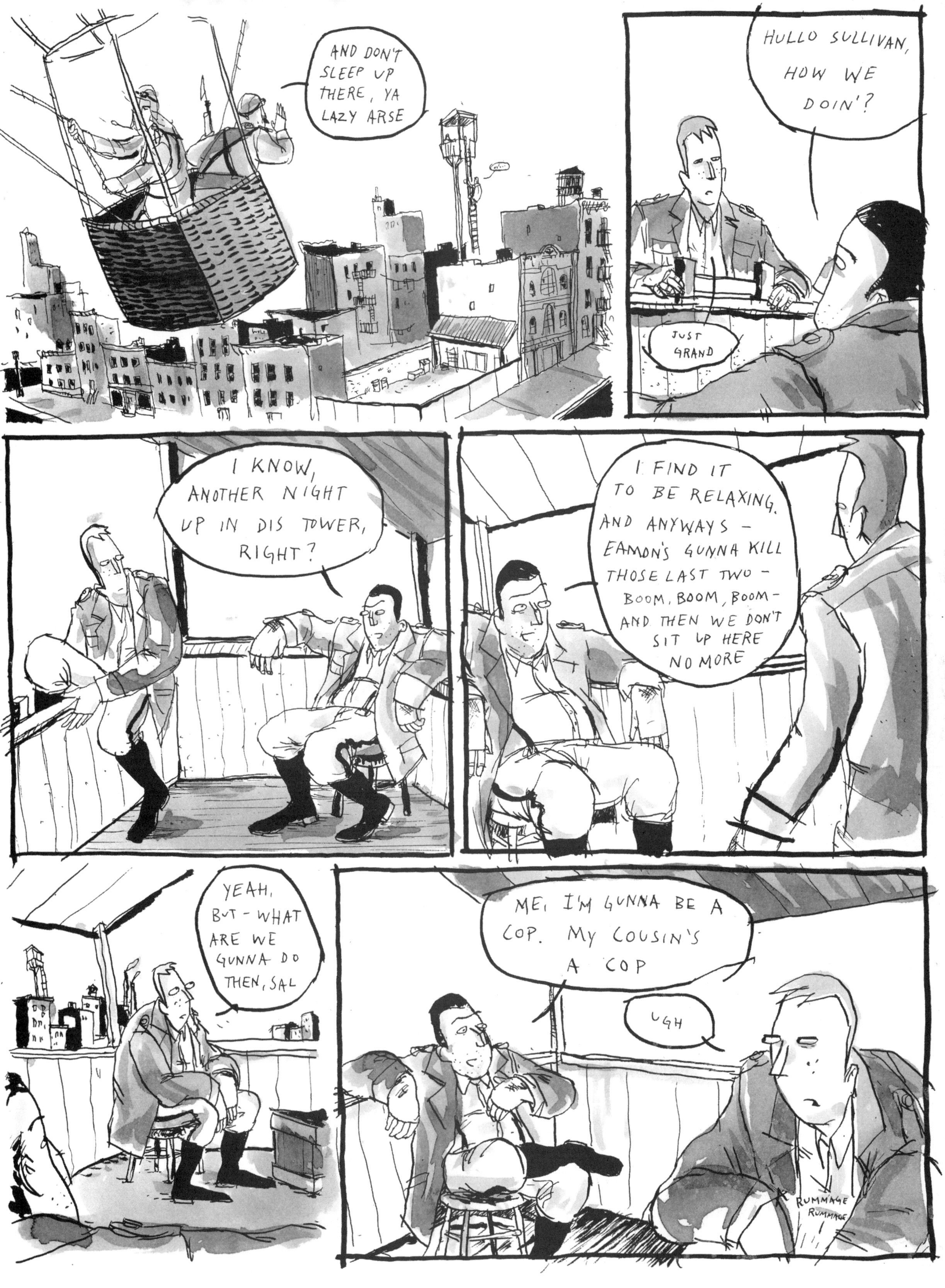
AND DON'T SLEEP UP THERE, YA LAZY ARSE
HULLO SULLIVAN, HOW WE DOIN'?
JUST GRAND
I KNOW, ANOTHER NIGHT UP IN DIS TOWER, RIGHT?
I FIND IT TO BE RELAXING. AND ANYWAYS – EAMON'S GUNNA KILL THOSE LAST TWO – BOOM, BOOM, BOOM – AND THEN WE DON'T SIT UP HERE NO MORE
YEAH, BUT – WHAT ARE WE GUNNA DO THEN, SAL
ME, I'M GUNNA BE A COP. MY COUSIN'S A COP
UGH
RUMMAGE RUMMAGE

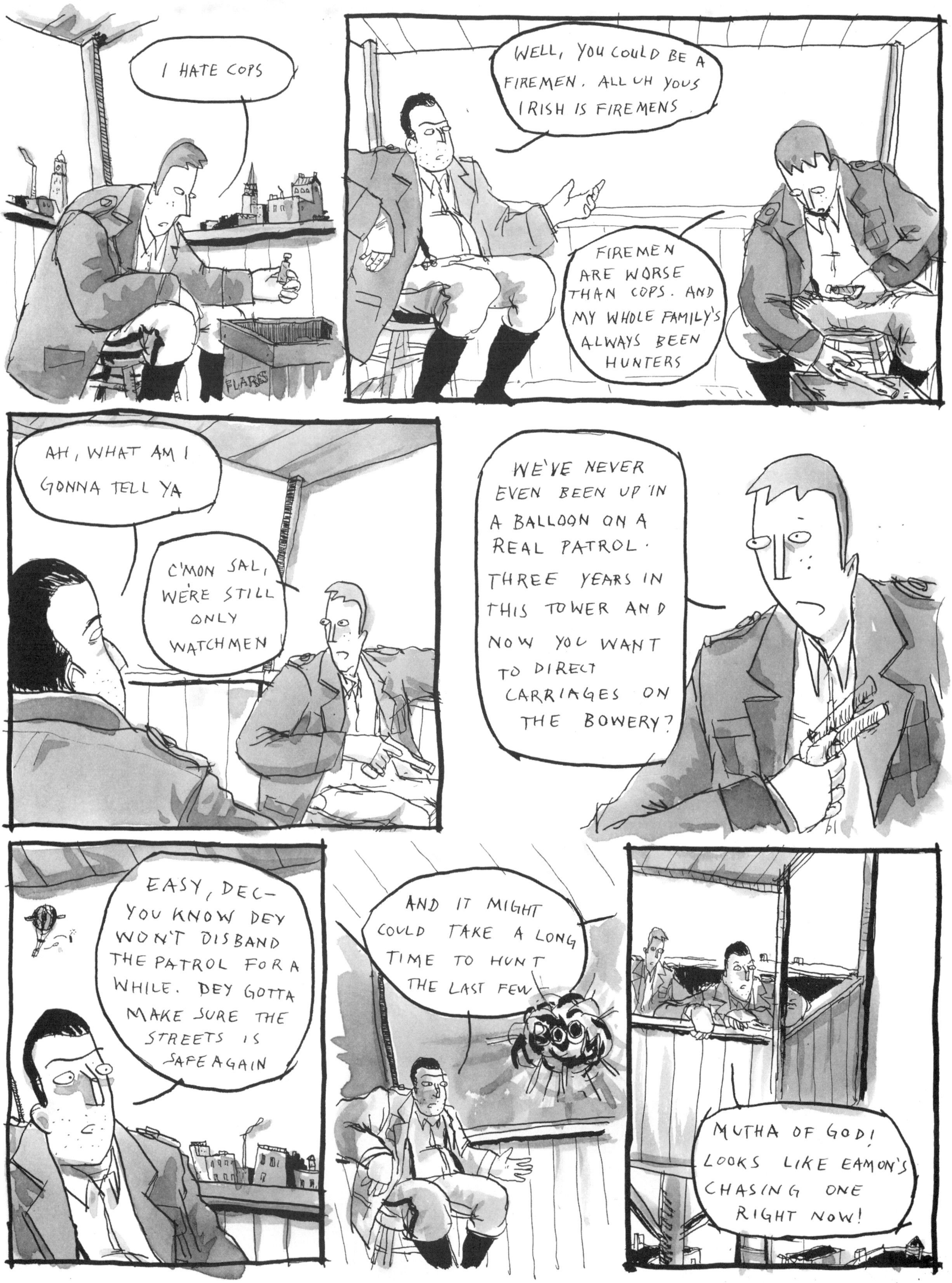
I HATE COPS
WELL, YOU COULD BE A FIREMEN. ALL UH YOUS IRISH IS FIREMENS
FIREMEN ARE WORSE THAN COPS. AND MY WHOLE FAMILY'S ALWAYS BEEN HUNTERS
FLARES
AH, WHAT AM I GONNA TELL YA
C'MON SAL, WE'RE STILL ONLY WATCHMEN
WE'VE NEVER EVEN BEEN UP IN A BALLOON ON A REAL PATROL. THREE YEARS IN THIS TOWER AND NOW YOU WANT TO DIRECT CARRIAGES ON THE BOWERY?
EASY, DEC- YOU KNOW DEY WON'T DISBAND THE PATROL FOR A WHILE. DEY GOTTA MAKE SURE THE STREETS IS SAFE AGAIN
AND IT MIGHT COULD TAKE A LONG TIME TO HUNT THE LAST FEW
MUTHA OF GOD! LOOKS LIKE EAMON'S CHASING ONE RIGHT NOW!

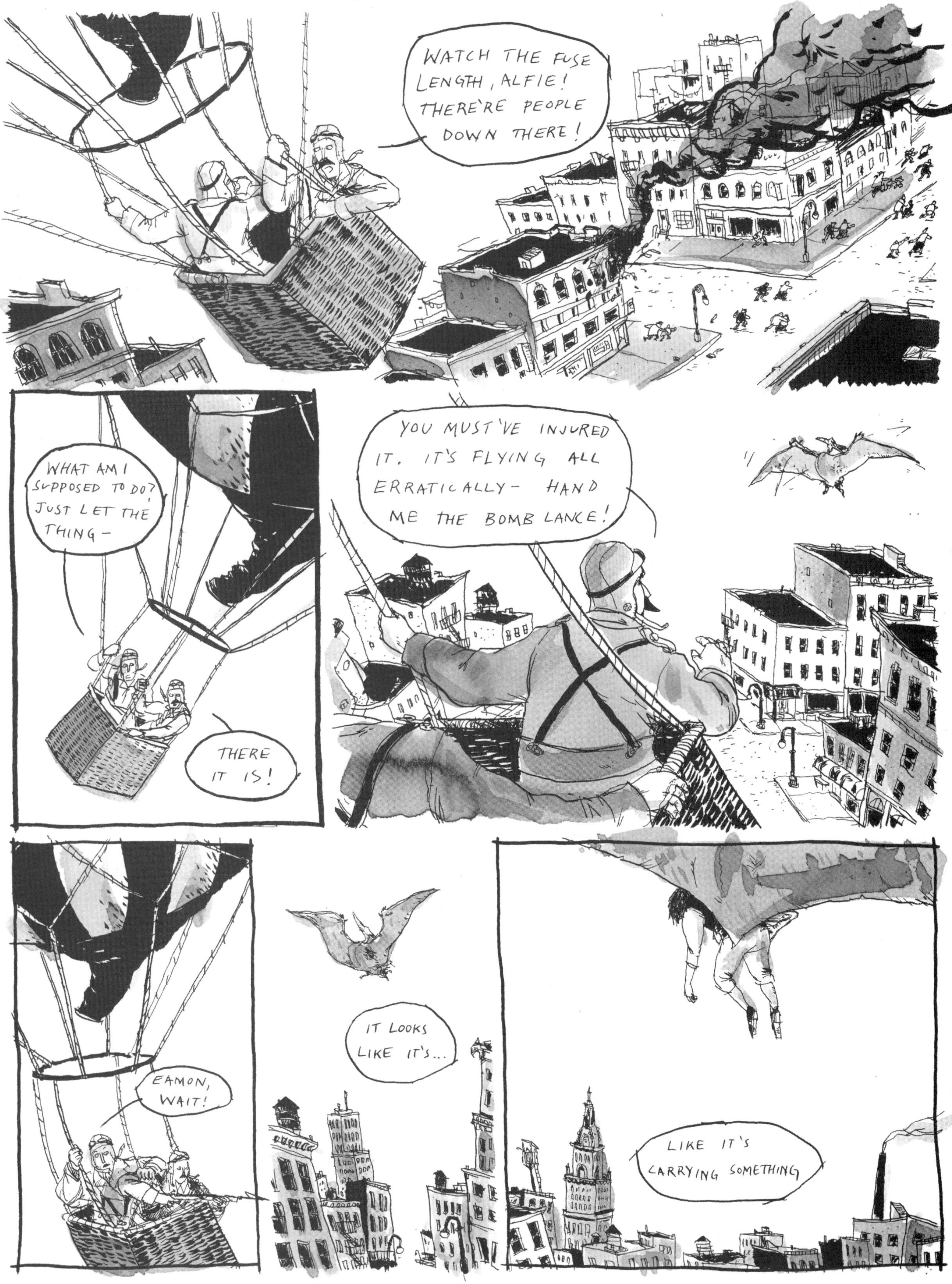
WATCH THE FUSE LENGTH, ALFIE! THERE'RE PEOPLE DOWN THERE!
WHAT AM I SUPPOSED TO DO? JUST LET THE THING-
THERE IT IS!
YOU MUST'VE INJURED IT. IT'S FLYING ALL ERRATICALLY- HAND ME THE BOMB LANCE!
EAMON, WAIT!
IT LOOKS LIKE IT'S...
LIKE IT'S CARRYING SOMETHING

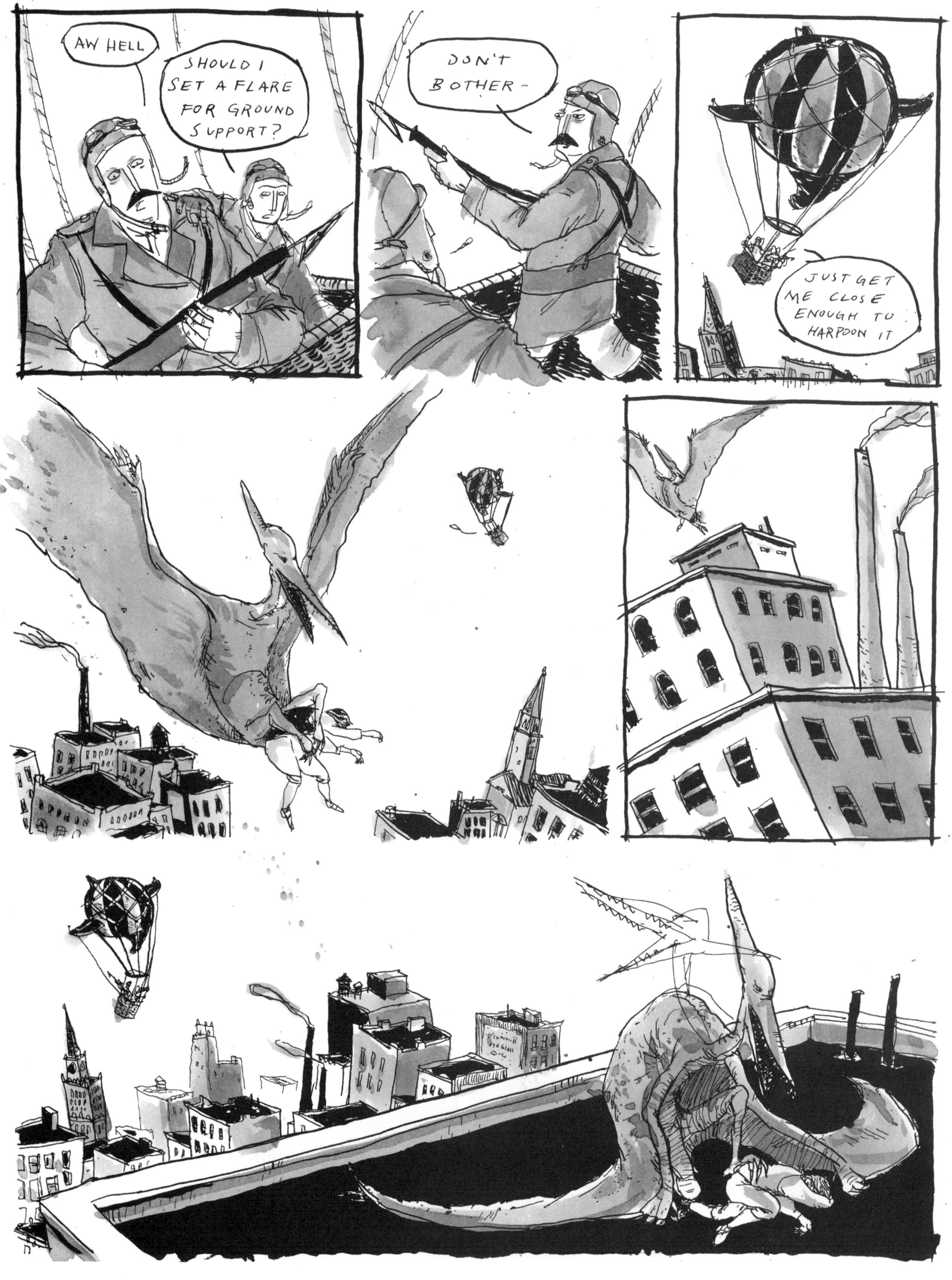
AW HELL
SHOULD I SET A FLARE FOR GROUND SUPPORT?
DON'T BOTHER-
JUST GET ME CLOSE ENOUGH TO HARPOON IT

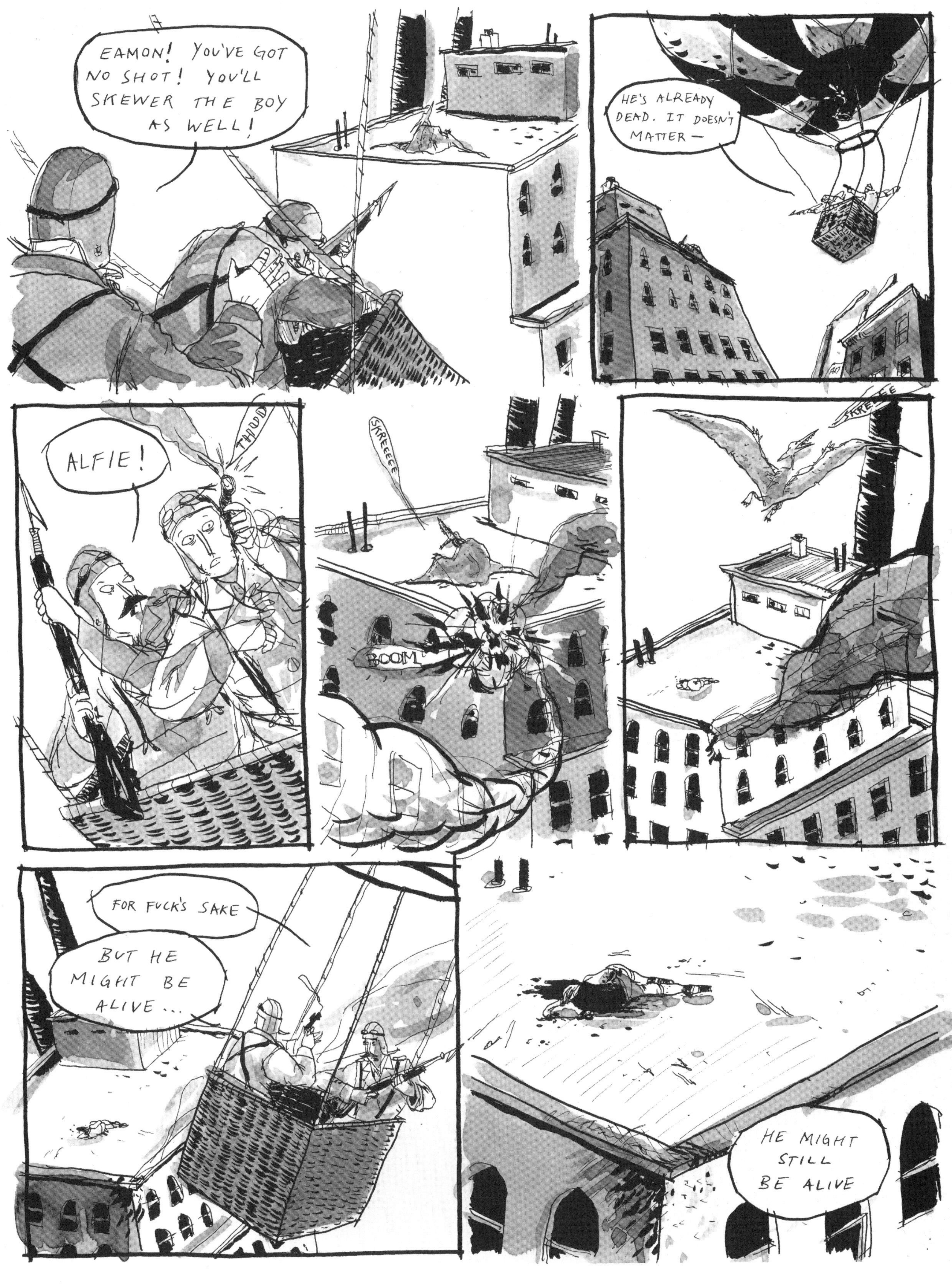
EAMON! YOU'VE GOT NO SHOT! YOU'LL SKEWER THE BOY AS WELL!
HE'S ALREADY DEAD. IT DOESN'T MATTER—
ALFIE!
THUD
SKREEEEE
BOOM
SKREEEEE
FOR FUCK'S SAKE
BUT HE MIGHT BE ALIVE...
HE MIGHT STILL BE ALIVE

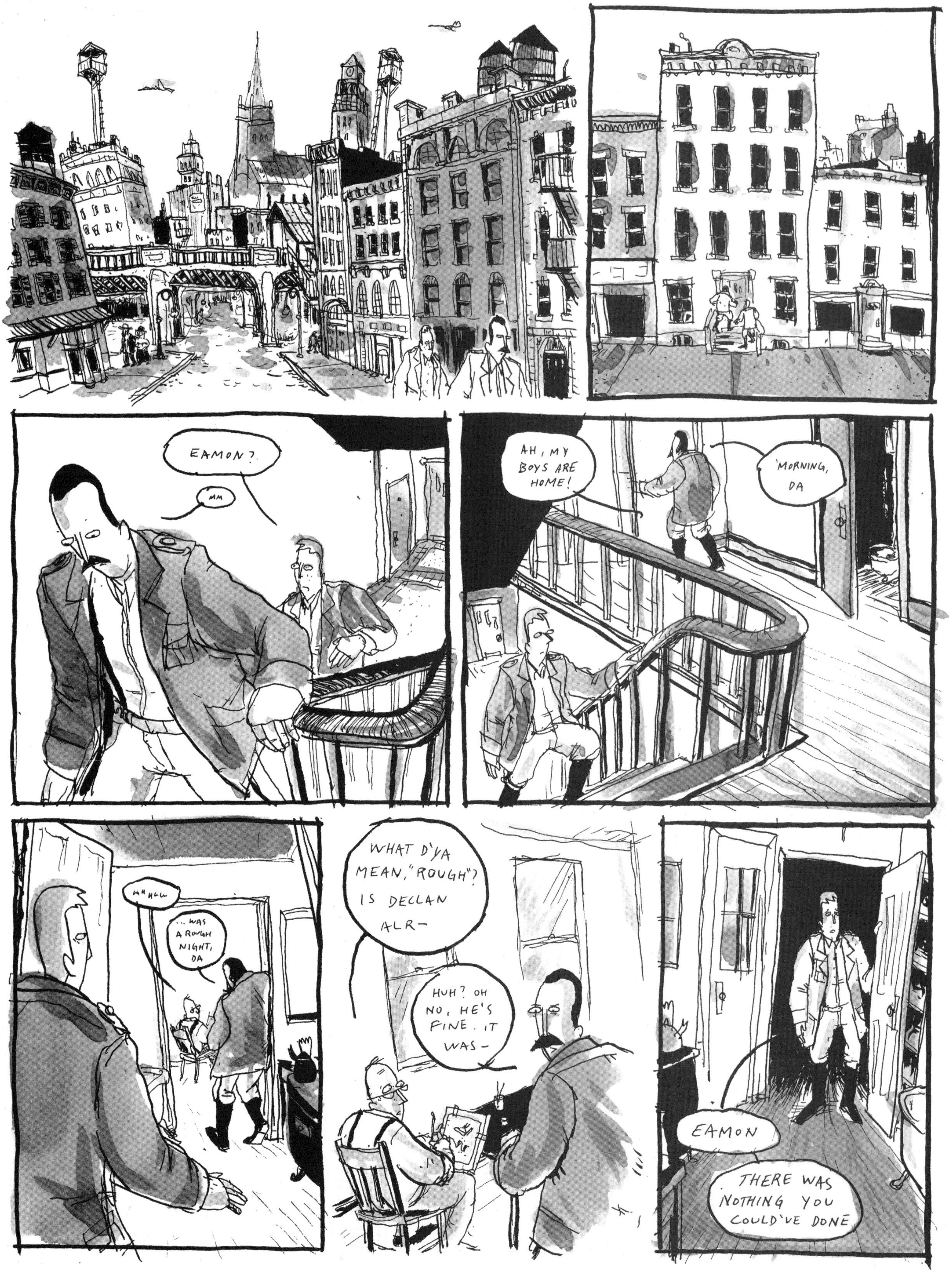
EAMON?
MM
AH, MY BOYS ARE HOME!
'MORNING, DA
...WAS A ROUGH NIGHT, DA
WHAT D'YA MEAN, "ROUGH"? IS DECLAN ALR—
HUH? OH NO, HE'S FINE. IT WAS—
EAMON
THERE WAS NOTHING YOU COULD'VE DONE

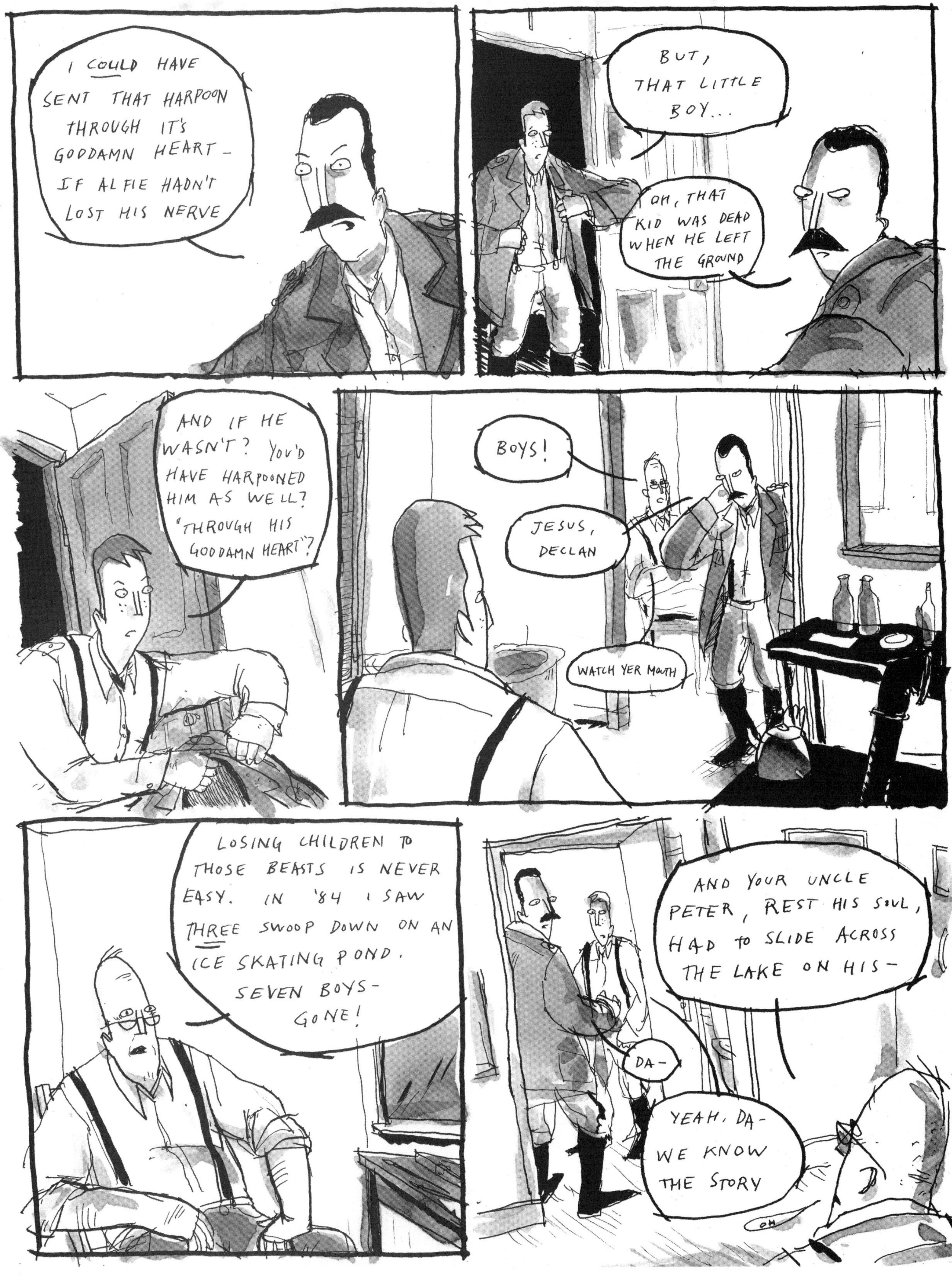
I COULD HAVE SENT THAT HARPOON THROUGH IT'S GODDAMN HEART - IF ALFIE HADN'T LOST HIS NERVE
BUT, THAT LITTLE BOY...
OH, THAT KID WAS DEAD WHEN HE LEFT THE GROUND
AND IF HE WASN'T? YOU'D HAVE HARPOONED HIM AS WELL? "THROUGH HIS GODDAMN HEART"?
BOYS!
JESUS, DECLAN
WATCH YER MOUTH
LOSING CHILDREN TO THOSE BEASTS IS NEVER EASY. IN '84 I SAW THREE SWOOP DOWN ON AN ICE SKATING POND. SEVEN BOYS - GONE!
AND YOUR UNCLE PETER, REST HIS SOUL, HAD TO SLIDE ACROSS THE LAKE ON HIS-
DA-
YEAH, DA - WE KNOW THE STORY
OH

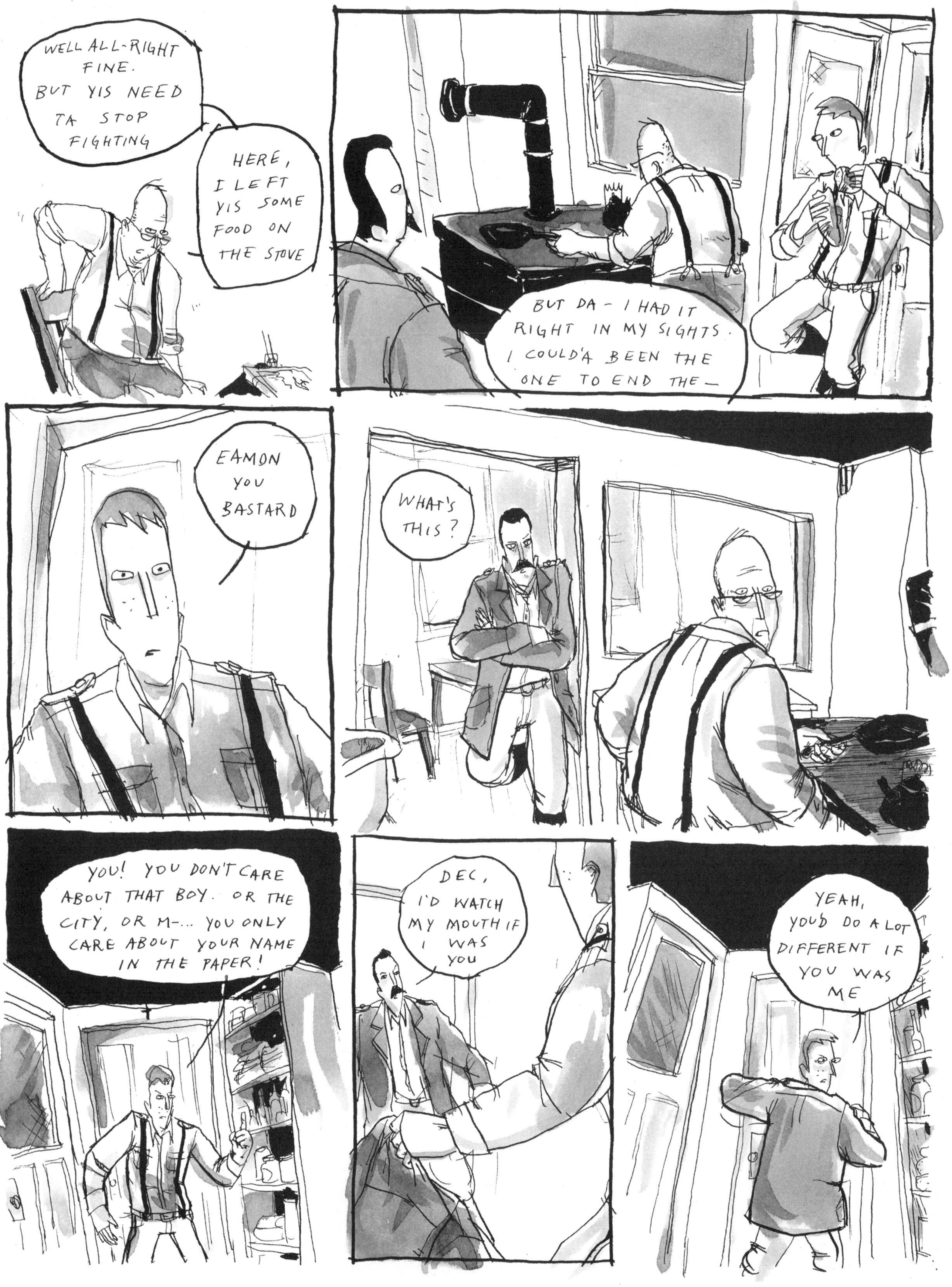
WELL ALL-RIGHT FINE. BUT YIS NEED TA STOP FIGHTING
HERE, I LEFT YIS SOME FOOD ON THE STOVE
BUT DA - I HAD IT RIGHT IN MY SIGHTS. I COULD'A BEEN THE ONE TO END THE—
EAMON YOU BASTARD
WHAT'S THIS?
YOU! YOU DON'T CARE ABOUT THAT BOY. OR THE CITY, OR M-... YOU ONLY CARE ABOUT YOUR NAME IN THE PAPER!
DEC, I'D WATCH MY MOUTH IF I WAS YOU
YEAH, YOU'D DO A LOT DIFFERENT IF YOU WAS ME

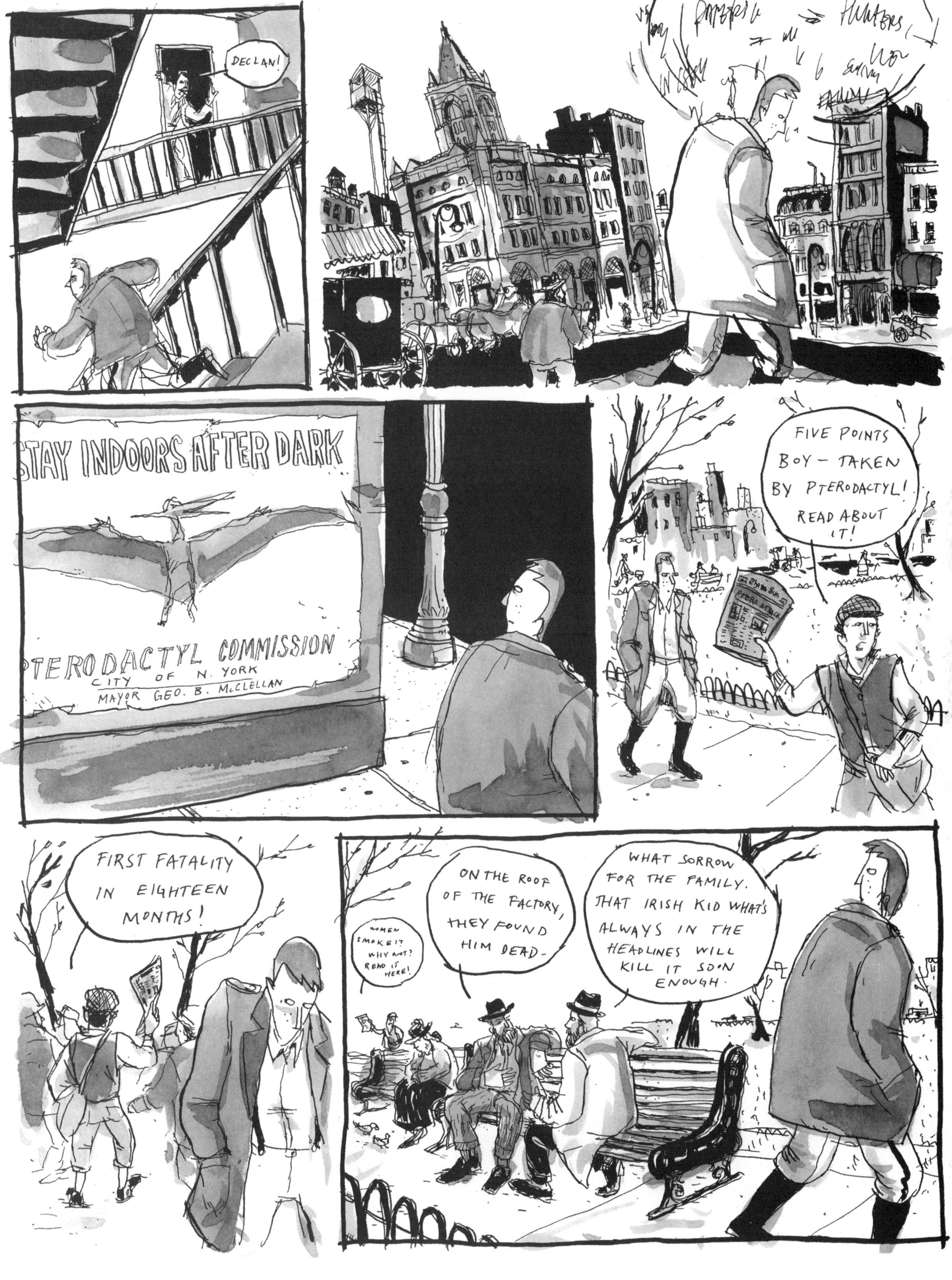
DECLAN!
STAY INDOORS AFTER DARK
PTERODACTYL COMMISSION
CITY OF N. YORK
MAYOR GEO. B. McCLELLAN
FIVE POINTS BOY - TAKEN BY PTERODACTYL! READ ABOUT IT!
FIRST FATALITY IN EIGHTEEN MONTHS!
WOMEN SMOKE IT WHY NOT? READ IT HERE!
ON THE ROOF OF THE FACTORY, THEY FOUND HIM DEAD-
WHAT SORROW FOR THE FAMILY. THAT IRISH KID WHAT'S ALWAYS IN THE HEADLINES WILL KILL IT SOON ENOUGH.

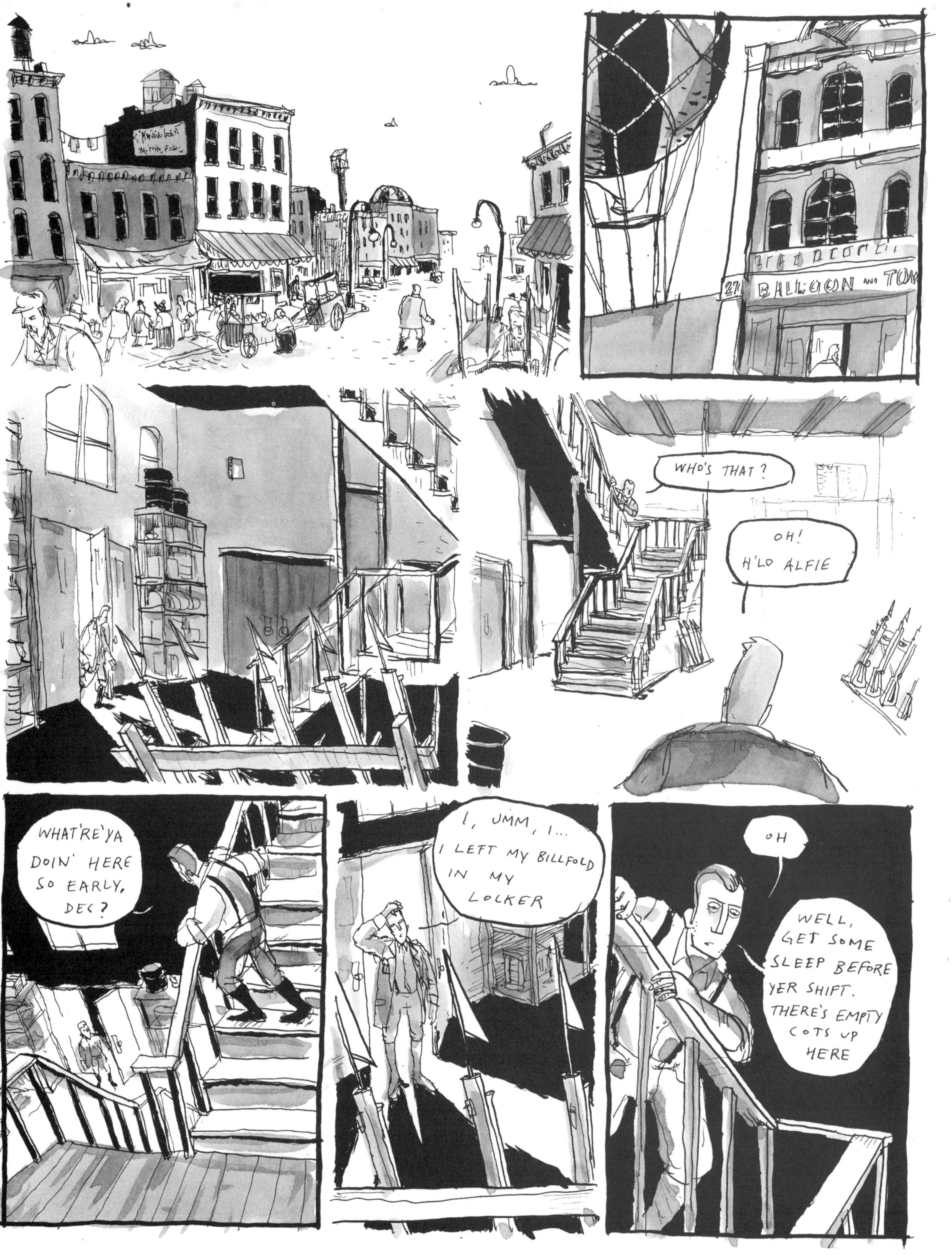

27
BALLOON AND TOW
WHO'S THAT?
OH! H'LO ALFIE
WHAT'RE'YA DOIN' HERE SO EARLY, DEC?
I, UMM, I... I LEFT MY BILLFOLD IN MY LOCKER
OH
WELL, GET SOME SLEEP BEFORE YER SHIFT. THERE'S EMPTY COTS UP HERE

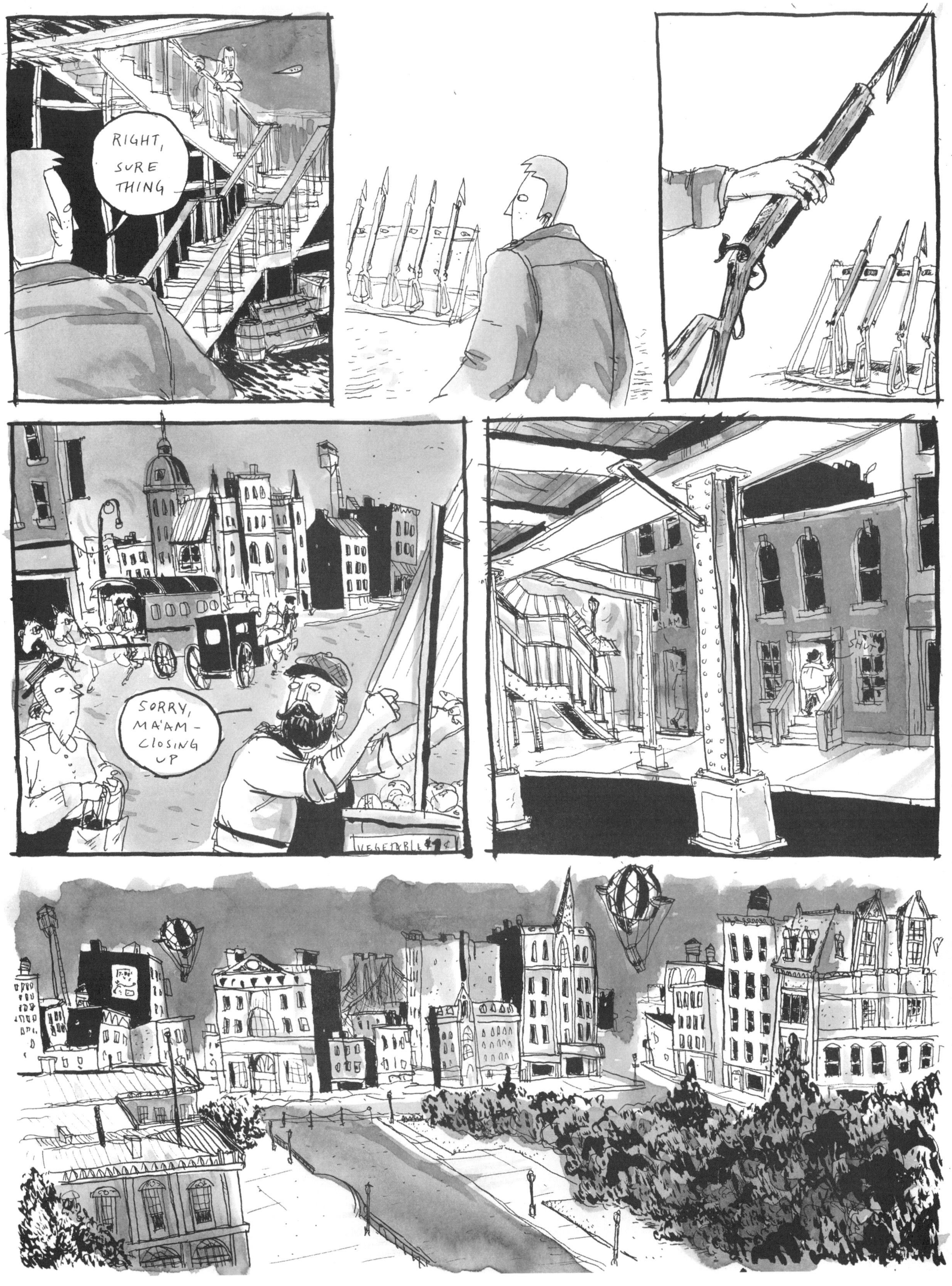
RIGHT, SURE THING
SORRY, MA'AM- CLOSING UP
VEGETABLE
SLAM
SHUT

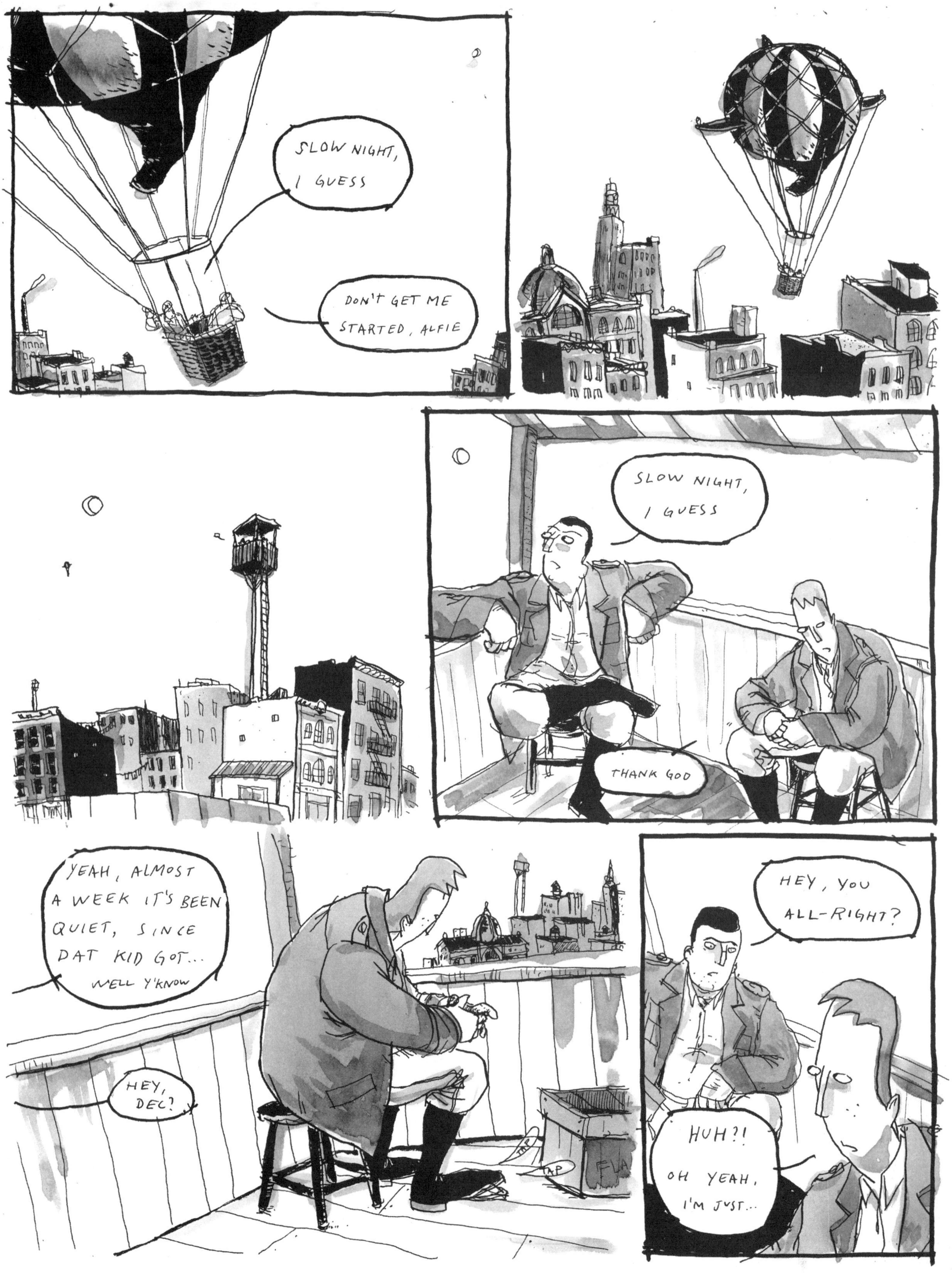
SLOW NIGHT, I GUESS
DON'T GET ME STARTED, ALFIE
SLOW NIGHT, I GUESS
THANK GOD
YEAH, ALMOST A WEEK IT'S BEEN QUIET, SINCE DAT KID GOT... WELL Y'KNOW
HEY, DEC?
TAP
HEY, YOU ALL-RIGHT?
HUH?!
OH YEAH, I'M JUST...

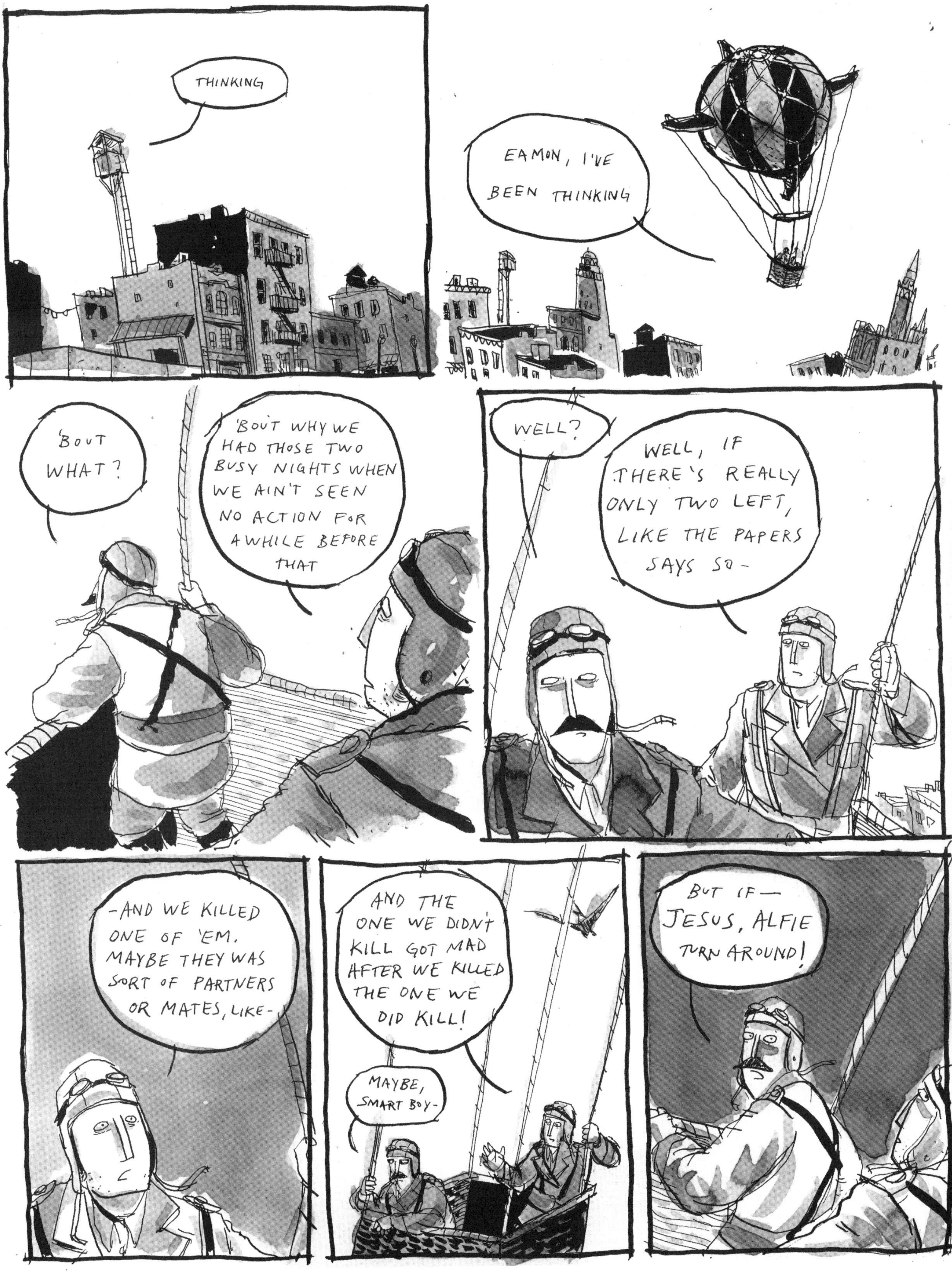
THINKING
EAMON, I'VE BEEN THINKING
'BOUT WHAT?
'BOUT WHY WE HAD THOSE TWO BUSY NIGHTS WHEN WE AIN'T SEEN NO ACTION FOR AWHILE BEFORE THAT
WELL?
WELL, IF THERE'S REALLY ONLY TWO LEFT, LIKE THE PAPERS SAYS SO-
-AND WE KILLED ONE OF 'EM. MAYBE THEY WAS SORT OF PARTNERS OR MATES, LIKE-
AND THE ONE WE DIDN'T KILL GOT MAD AFTER WE KILLED THE ONE WE DID KILL!
MAYBE, SMART BOY-
BUT IF— JESUS, ALFIE TURN AROUND!

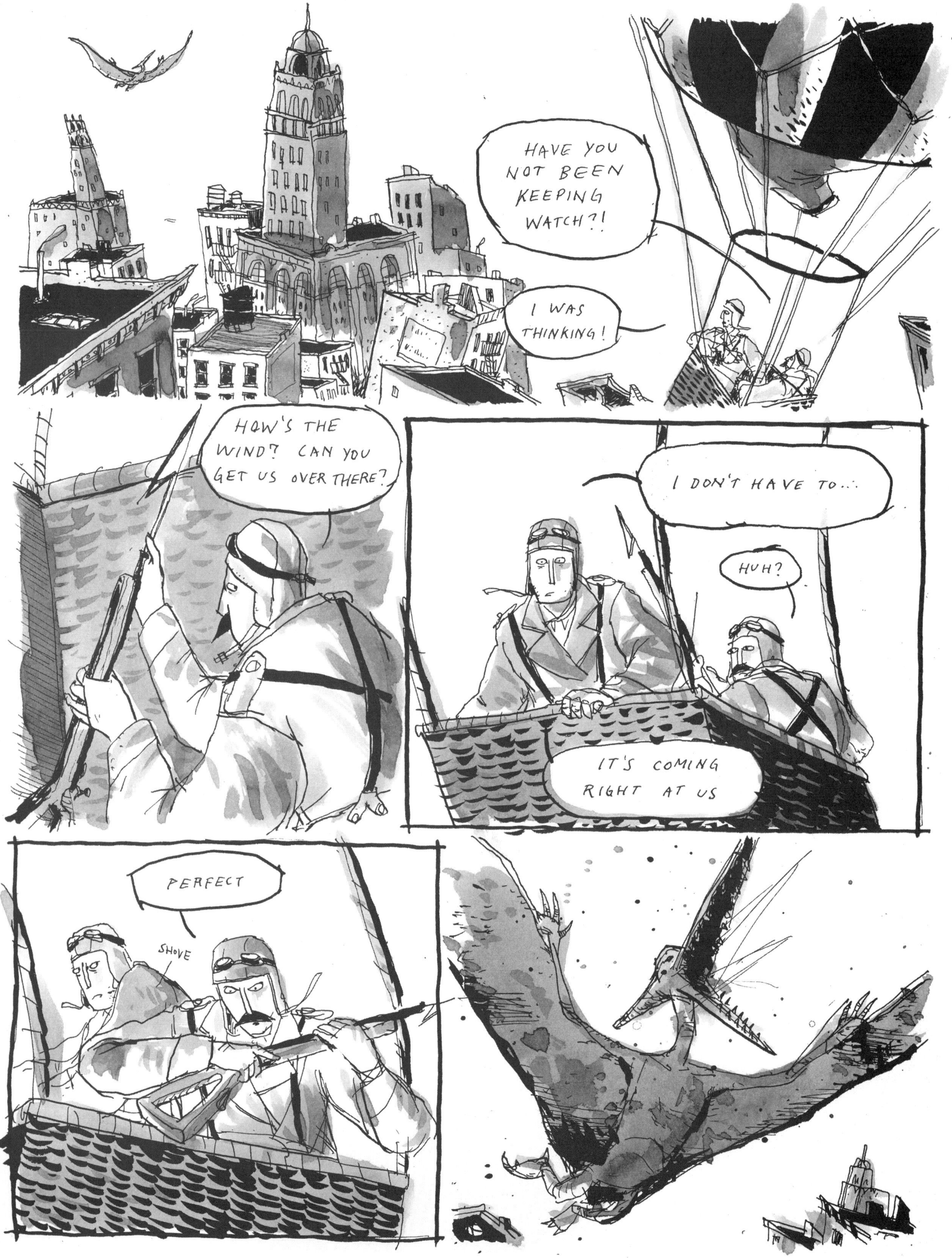
HAVE YOU NOT BEEN KEEPING WATCH?!
I WAS THINKING!
HOW'S THE WIND? CAN YOU GET US OVER THERE?
I DON'T HAVE TO...
HUH?
IT'S COMING RIGHT AT US
PERFECT
SHOVE

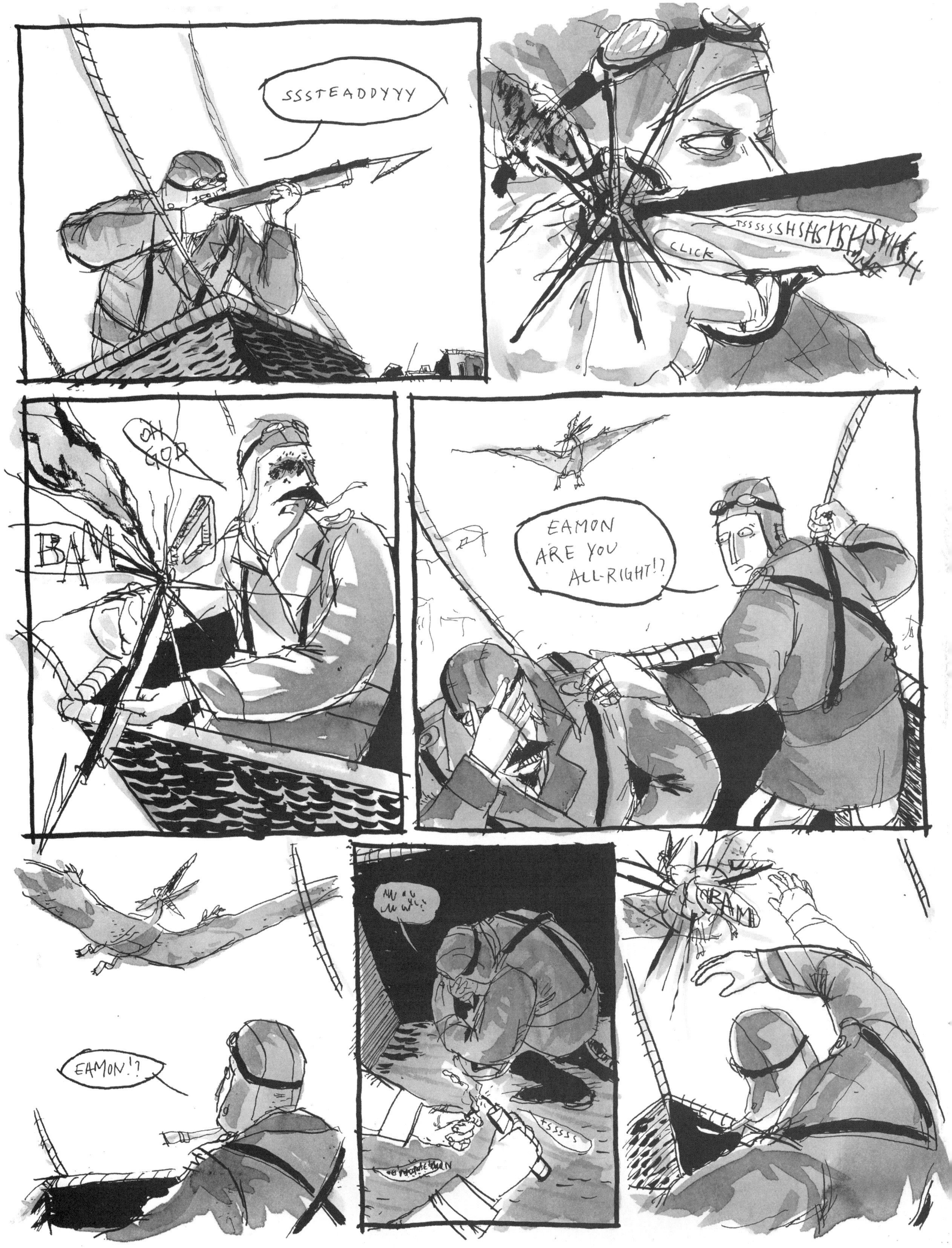
SSSTEADDYYY
TSSSSSSHSHS
CLICK
OH GOD
BAM
EAMON ARE YOU ALL-RIGHT!?
EAMON!?
BAM
TSSSSS

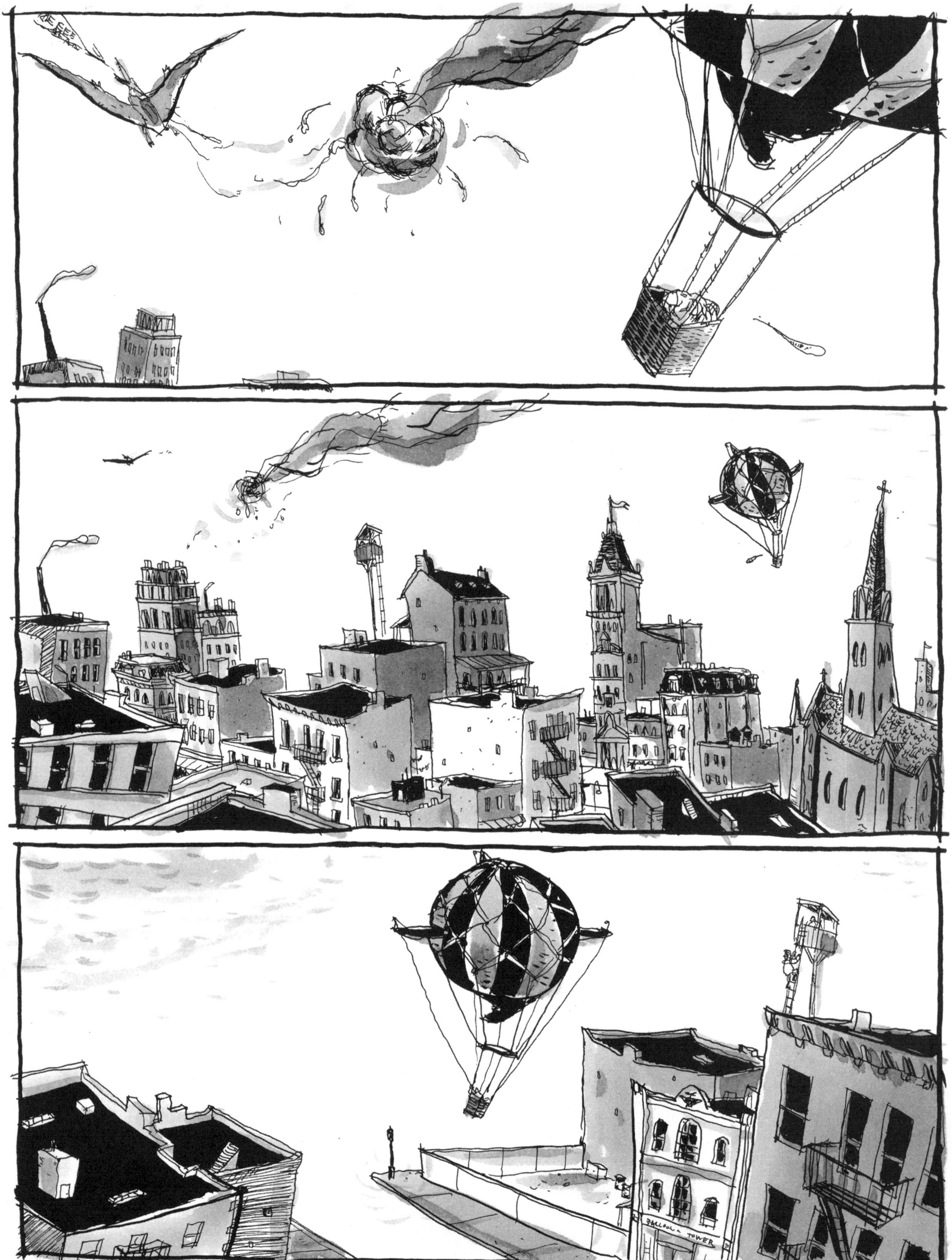
BALLOON TOWER

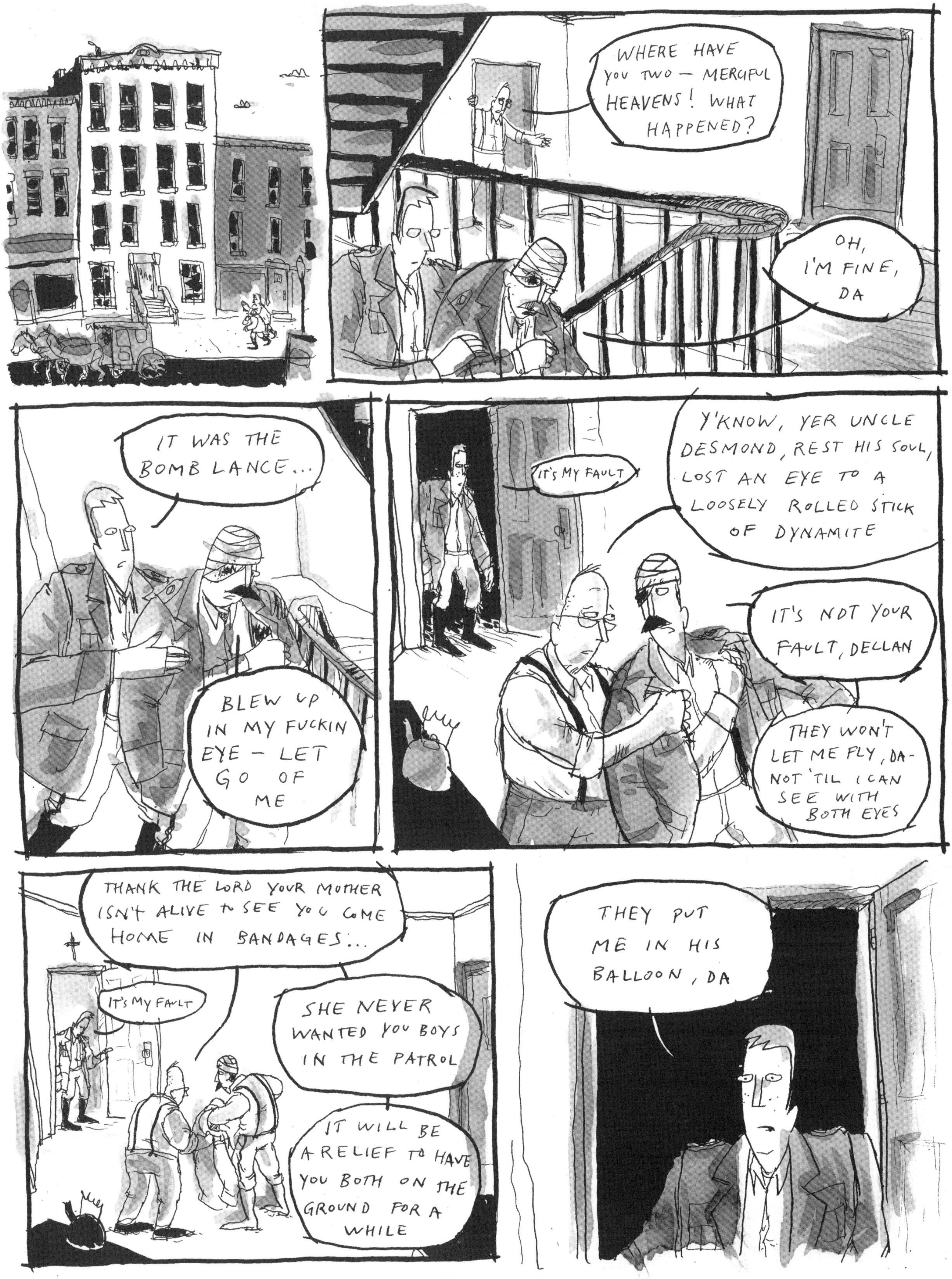
WHERE HAVE YOU TWO — MERCIFUL HEAVENS! WHAT HAPPENED?
OH, I'M FINE, DA
IT WAS THE BOMB LANCE...
BLEW UP IN MY FUCKIN EYE — LET GO OF ME
IT'S MY FAULT
Y'KNOW, YER UNCLE DESMOND, REST HIS SOUL, LOST AN EYE TO A LOOSELY ROLLED STICK OF DYNAMITE
IT'S NOT YOUR FAULT, DELLAN
THEY WON'T LET ME FLY, DA — NOT 'TIL I CAN SEE WITH BOTH EYES
THANK THE LORD YOUR MOTHER ISN'T ALIVE TO SEE YOU COME HOME IN BANDAGES...
IT'S MY FAULT
SHE NEVER WANTED YOU BOYS IN THE PATROL
IT WILL BE A RELIEF TO HAVE YOU BOTH ON THE GROUND FOR A WHILE
THEY PUT ME IN HIS BALLOON, DA

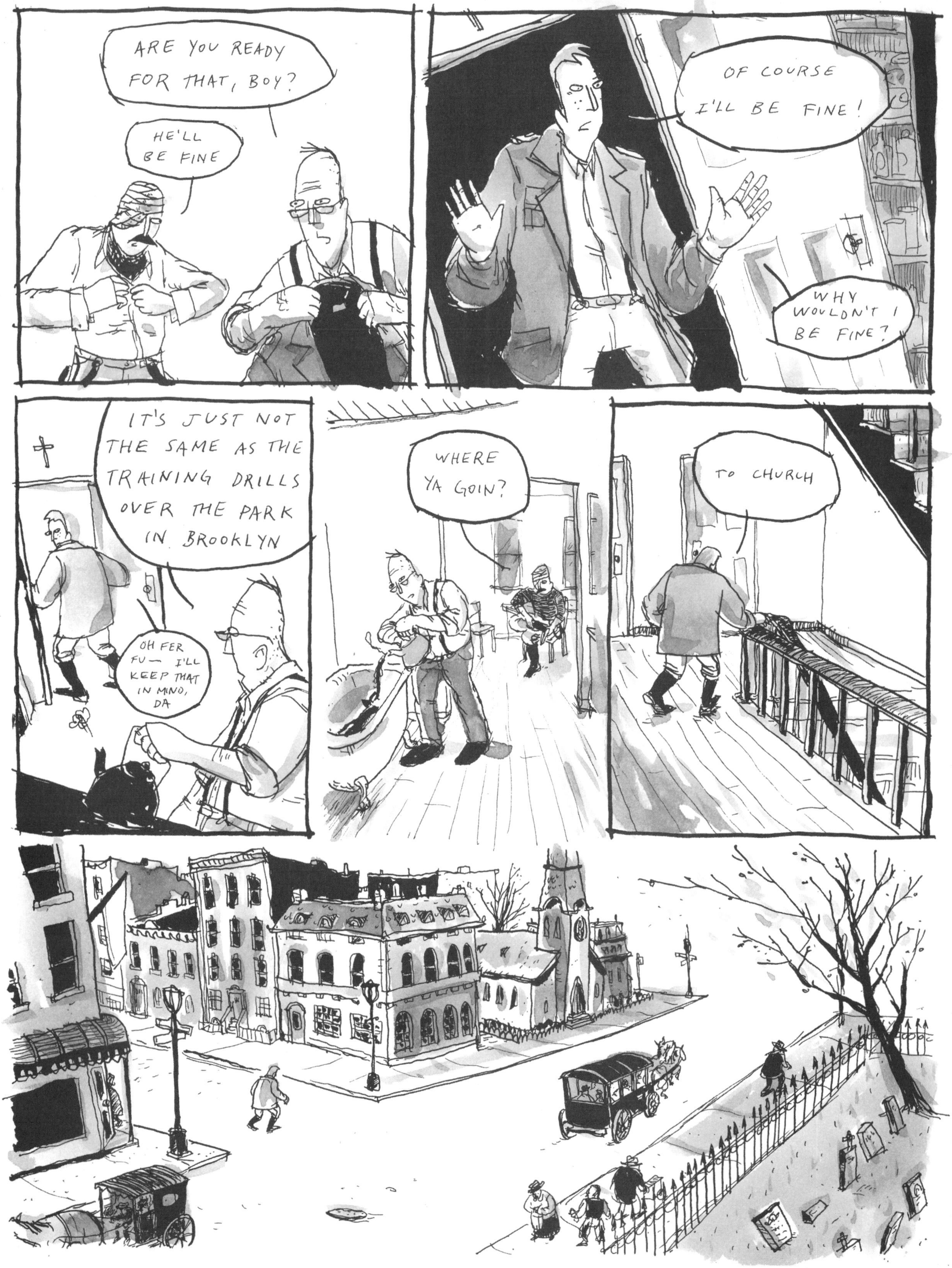
ARE YOU READY FOR THAT, BOY?
HE'LL BE FINE
OF COURSE I'LL BE FINE!
WHY WOULDN'T I BE FINE?
IT'S JUST NOT THE SAME AS THE TRAINING DRILLS OVER THE PARK IN BROOKLYN
OH FER FU— I'LL KEEP THAT IN MIND, DA
WHERE YA GOIN?
TO CHURCH

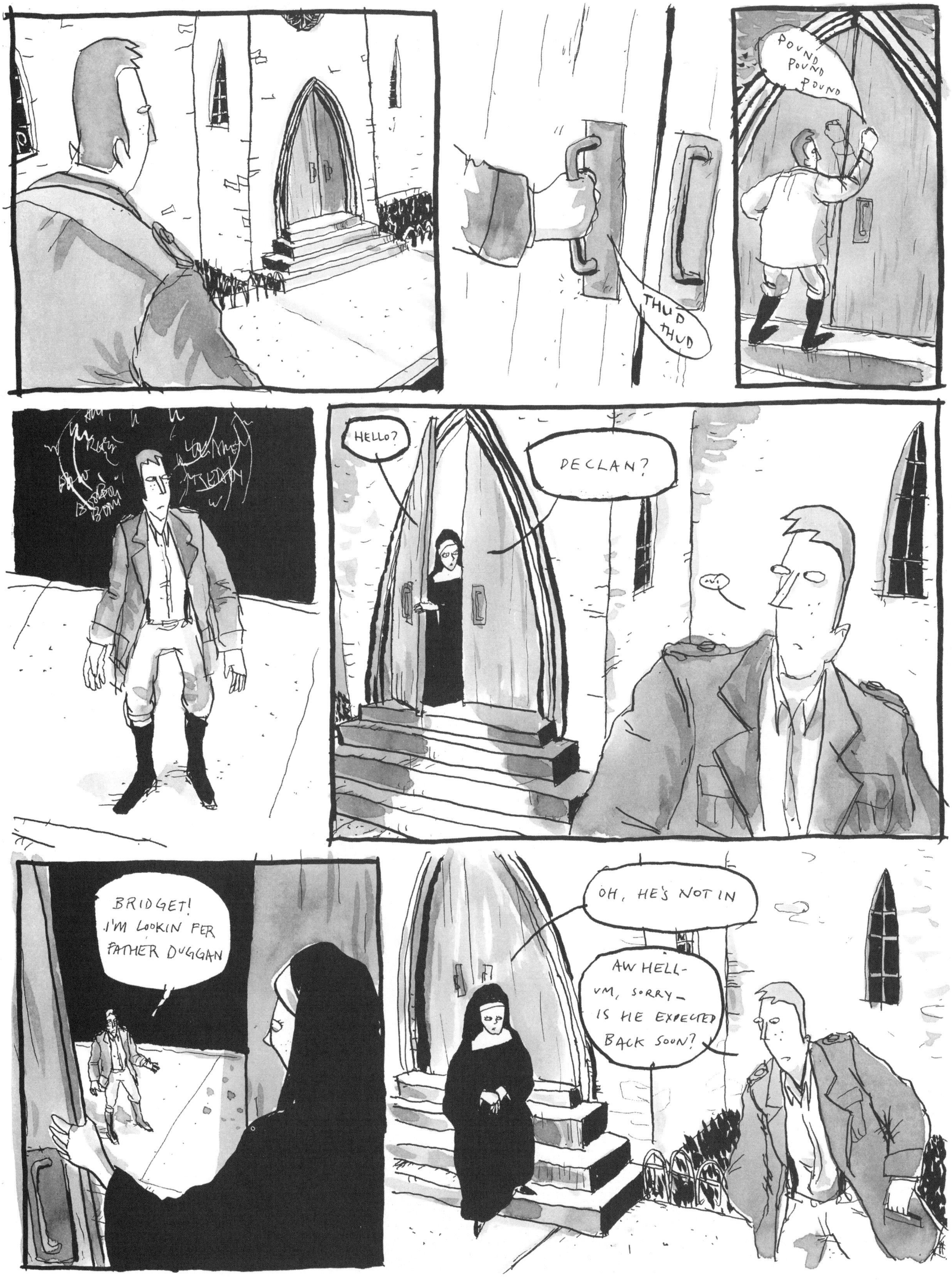
THUD THUD
POUND POUND POUND
HELLO?
DECLAN?
BRIDGET! I'M LOOKIN FER FATHER DUGGAN
OH, HE'S NOT IN
AW HELL- UM, SORRY- IS HE EXPECTED BACK SOON?

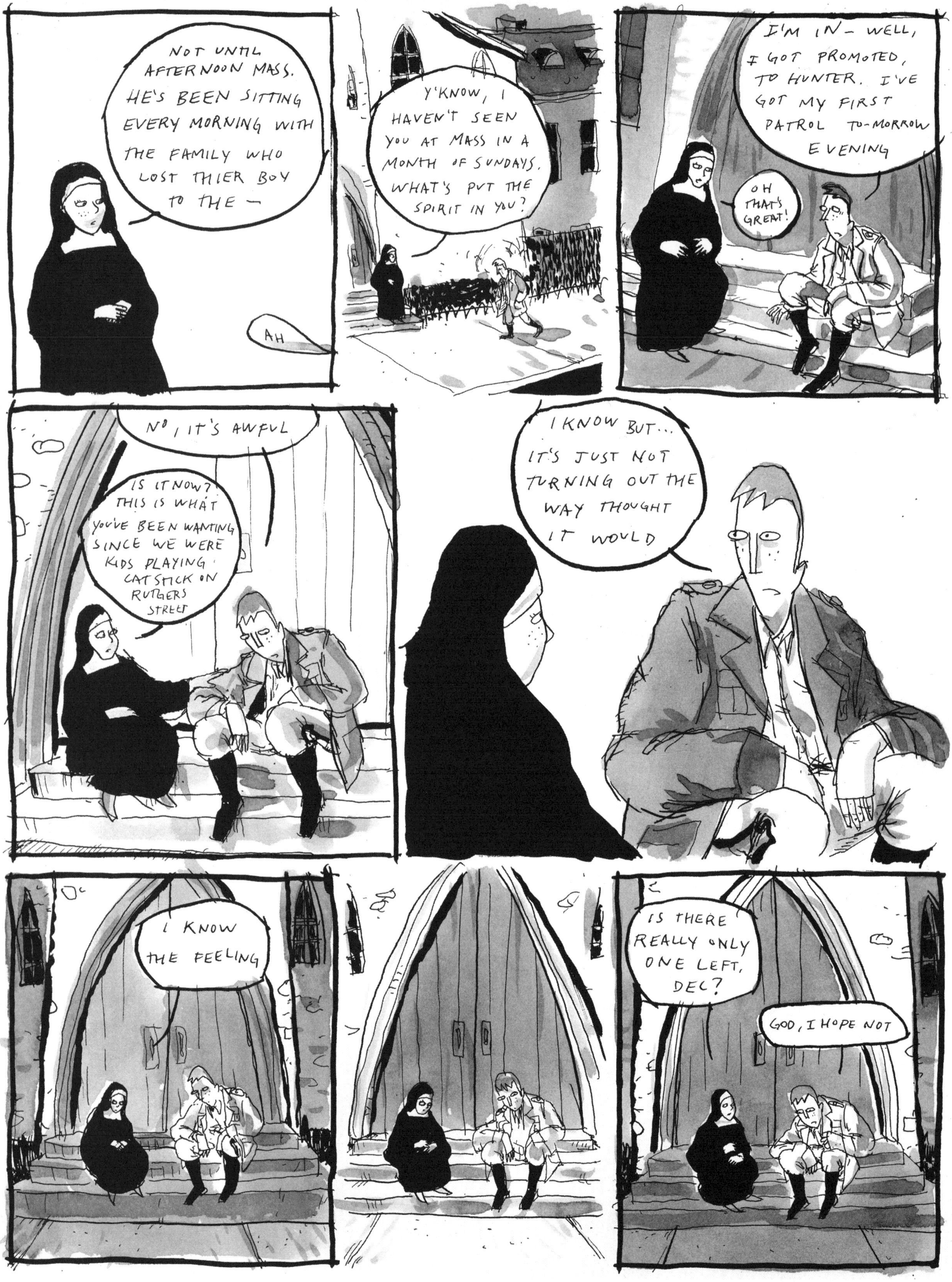
NOT UNTIL AFTERNOON MASS. HE'S BEEN SITTING EVERY MORNING WITH THE FAMILY WHO LOST THIER BOY TO THE —
AH
Y'KNOW, I HAVEN'T SEEN YOU AT MASS IN A MONTH OF SUNDAYS. WHAT'S PUT THE SPIRIT IN YOU?
I'M IN — WELL, I GOT PROMOTED, TO HUNTER. I'VE GOT MY FIRST PATROL TO-MORROW EVENING
OH THAT'S GREAT!
NO, IT'S AWFUL
IS IT NOW? THIS IS WHAT YOU'VE BEEN WANTING SINCE WE WERE KIDS PLAYING CAT STICK ON RUTGERS STREET
I KNOW BUT... IT'S JUST NOT TURNING OUT THE WAY THOUGHT IT WOULD
I KNOW THE FEELING
IS THERE REALLY ONLY ONE LEFT, DEC?
GOD, I HOPE NOT

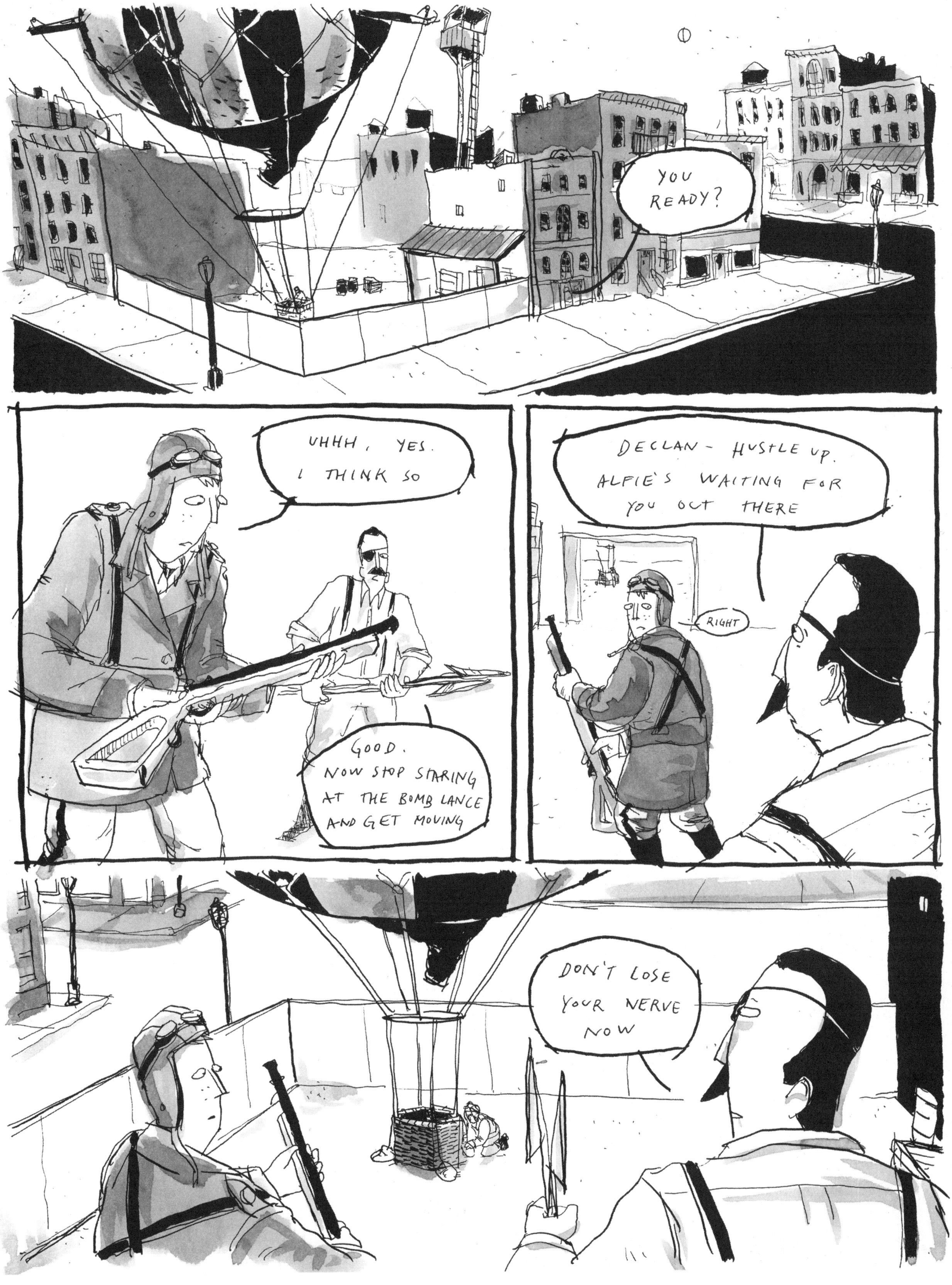
YOU READY?
UHHH, YES. I THINK SO
GOOD. NOW STOP STARING AT THE BOMB LANCE AND GET MOVING
DECLAN- HUSTLE UP. ALFIE'S WAITING FOR YOU OUT THERE
RIGHT
DON'T LOSE YOUR NERVE NOW

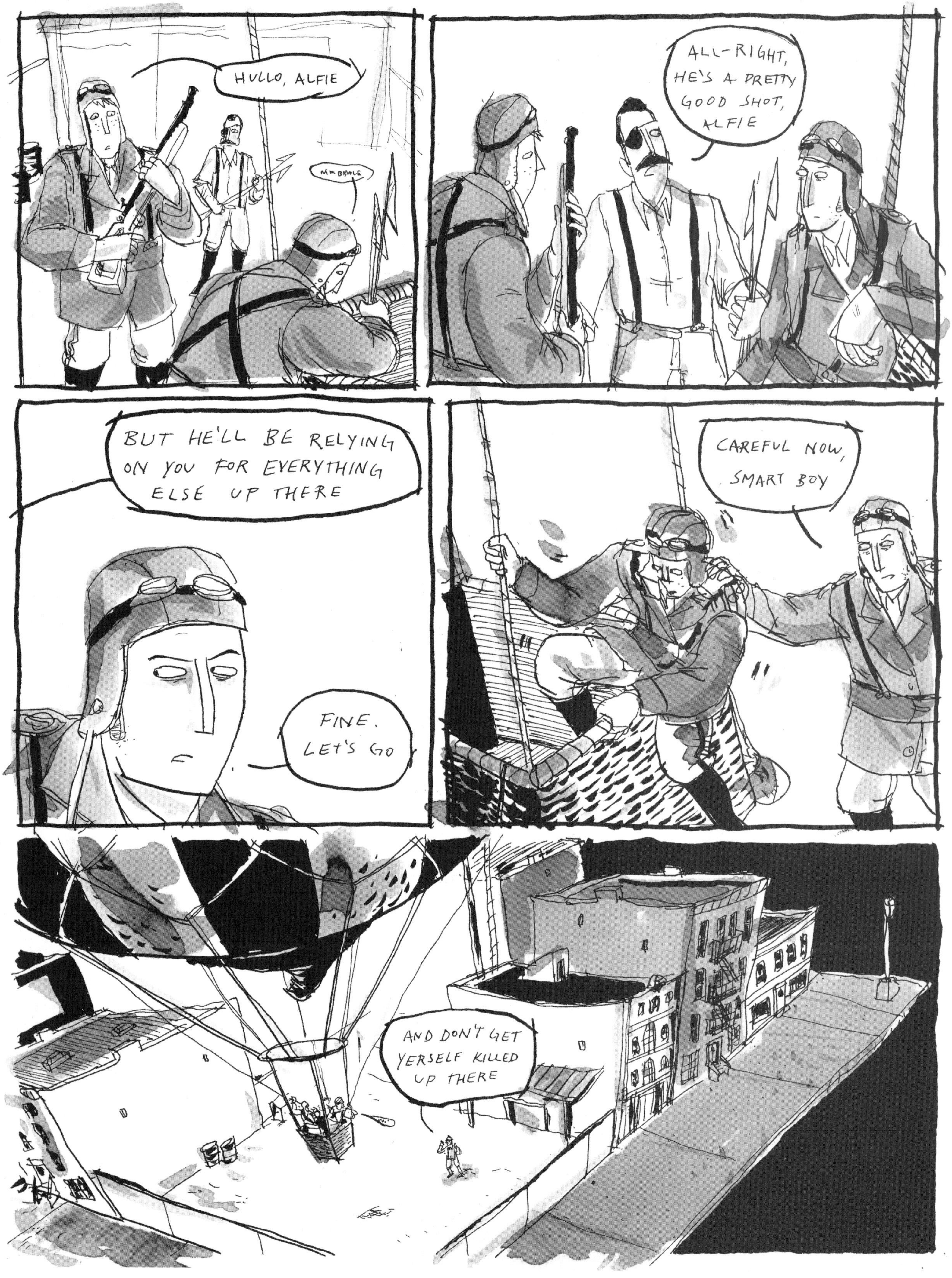
HULLO, ALFIE
MMBRWLE
ALL-RIGHT, HE'S A PRETTY GOOD SHOT, ALFIE
BUT HE'LL BE RELYING ON YOU FOR EVERYTHING ELSE UP THERE
FINE. LET'S GO
CAREFUL NOW, SMART BOY
AND DON'T GET YERSELF KILLED UP THERE

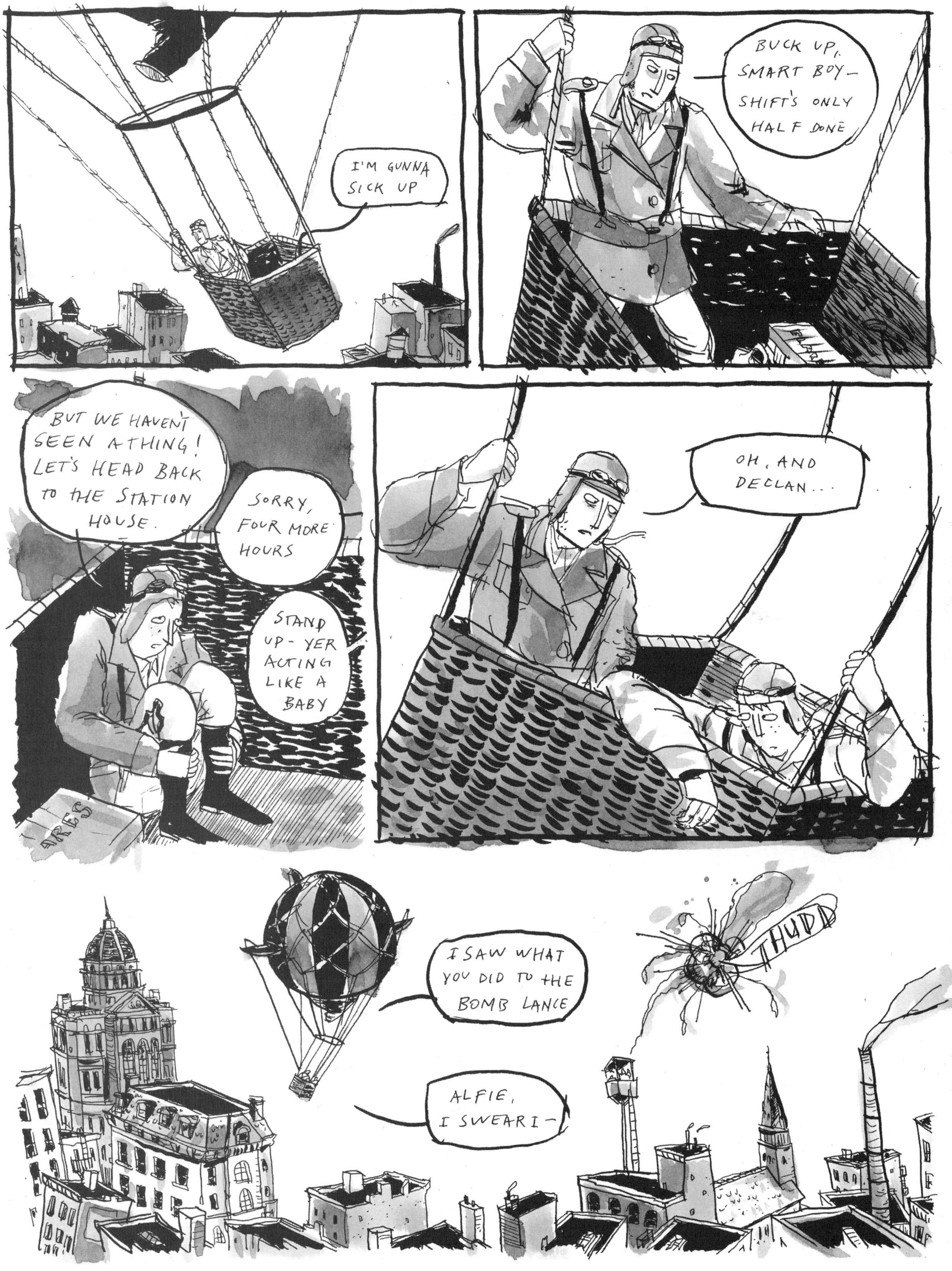
I'M GUNNA SICK UP
BUCK UP, SMART BOY— SHIFT'S ONLY HALF DONE
BUT WE HAVEN'T SEEN A THING! LET'S HEAD BACK TO THE STATION HOUSE.
SORRY, FOUR MORE HOURS
STAND UP- YER ACTING LIKE A BABY
OH, AND DECLAN...
I SAW WHAT YOU DID TO THE BOMB LANCE
THUDD
ALFIE, I SWEAR I—

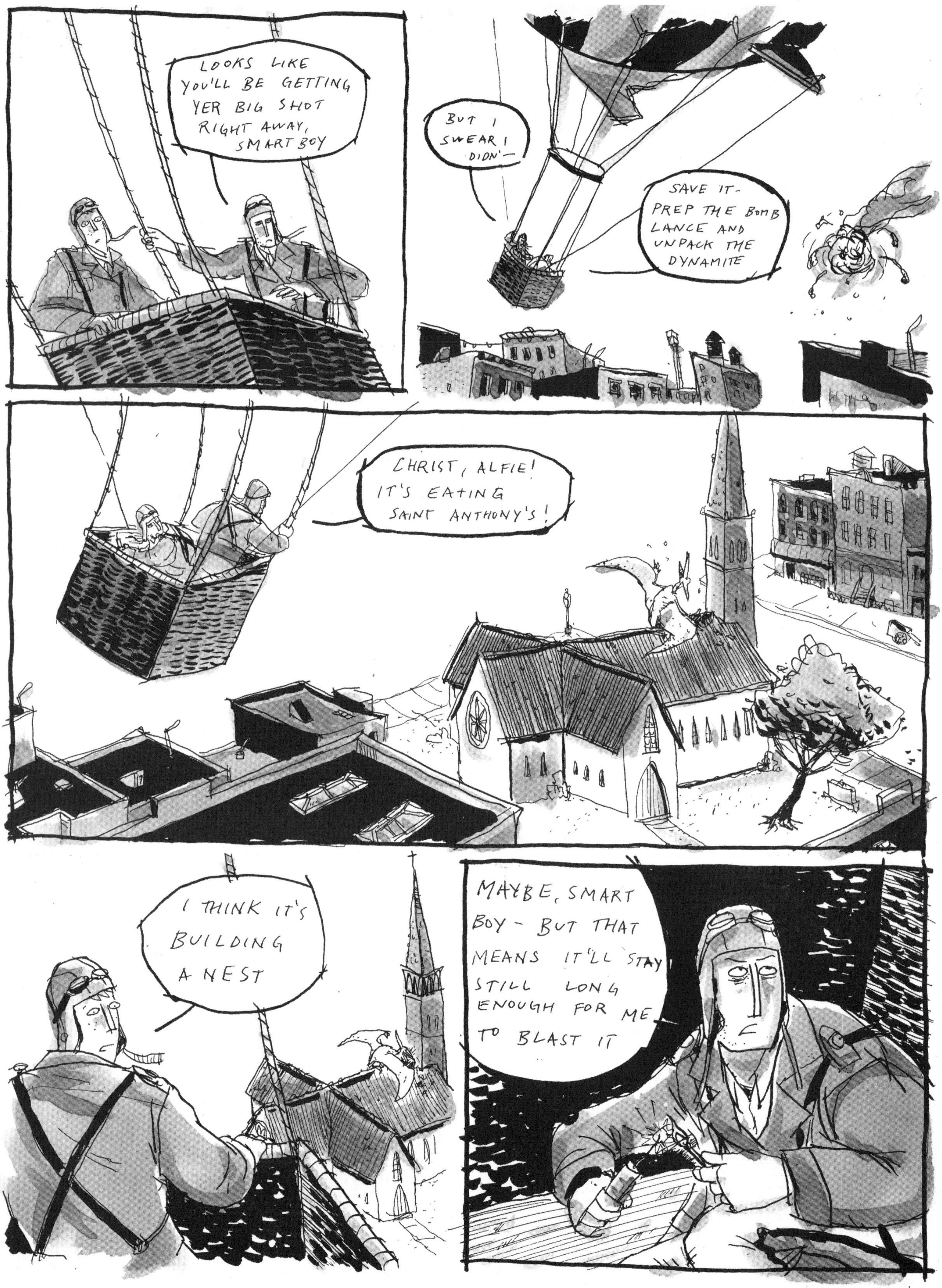
LOOKS LIKE YOU'LL BE GETTING YER BIG SHOT RIGHT AWAY, SMART BOY
BUT I SWEAR I DIDN'-
SAVE IT- PREP THE BOMB LANCE AND UNPACK THE DYNAMITE
CHRIST, ALFIE! IT'S EATING SAINT ANTHONY'S!
I THINK IT'S BUILDING A NEST
MAYBE, SMART BOY - BUT THAT MEANS IT'LL STAY STILL LONG ENOUGH FOR ME TO BLAST IT

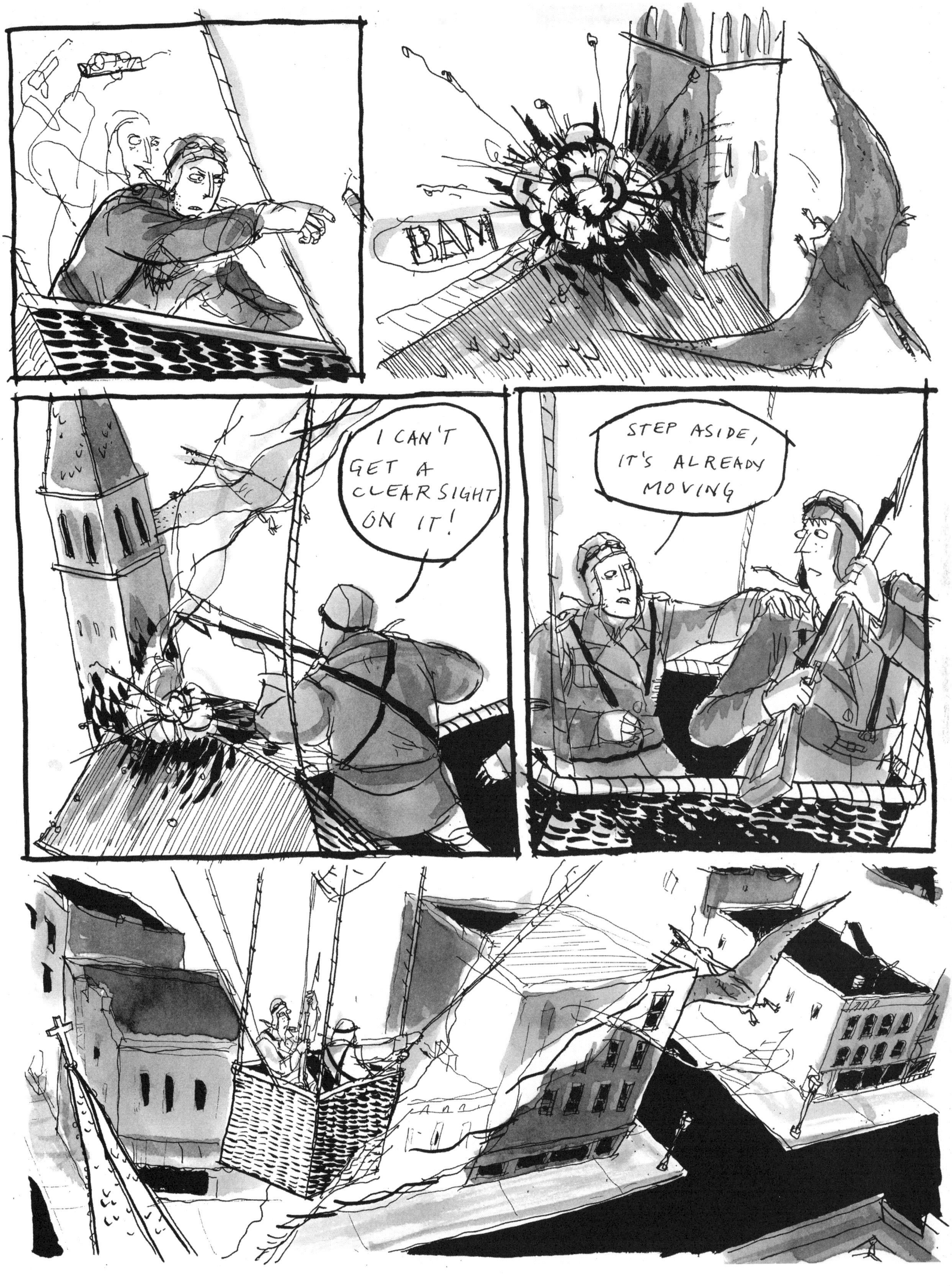
BAM
I CAN'T GET A CLEAR SIGHT ON IT!
STEP ASIDE, IT'S ALREADY MOVING

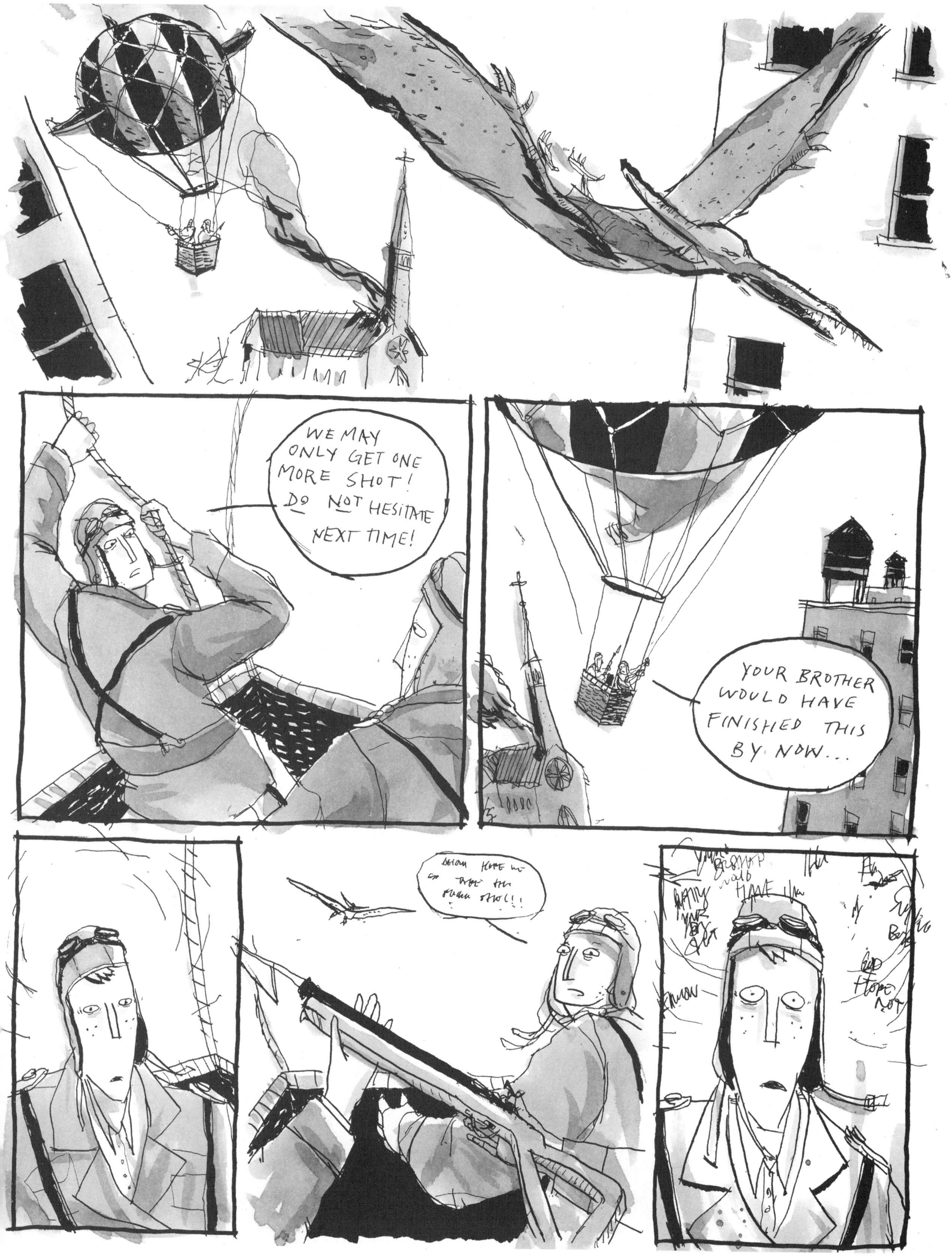
WE MAY ONLY GET ONE MORE SHOT! DO NOT HESITATE NEXT TIME!
YOUR BROTHER WOULD HAVE FINISHED THIS BY NOW...

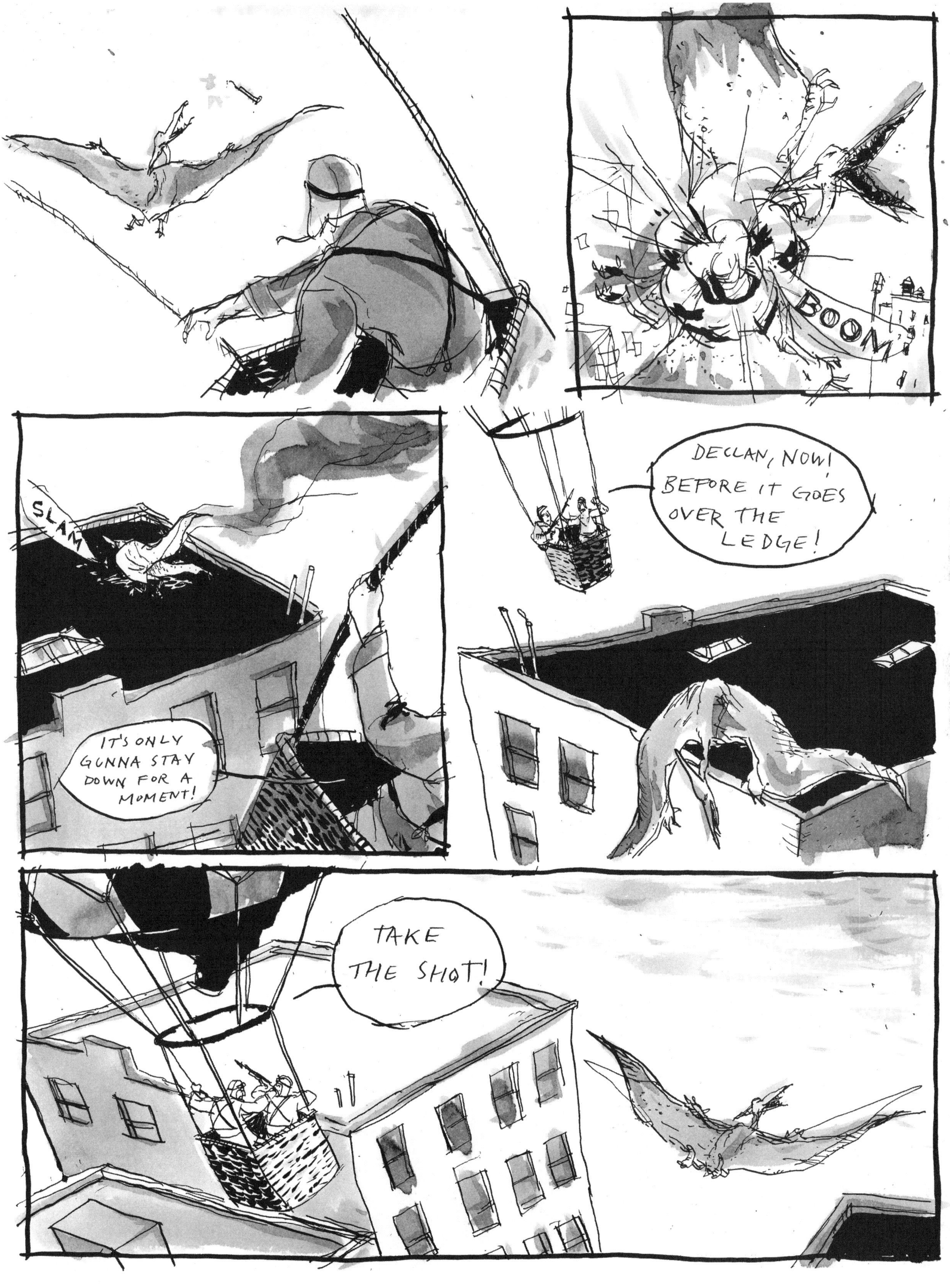
BOOM
SLAM
IT'S ONLY GUNNA STAY DOWN FOR A MOMENT!
DECLAN, NOW! BEFORE IT GOES OVER THE LEDGE!
TAKE THE SHOT!

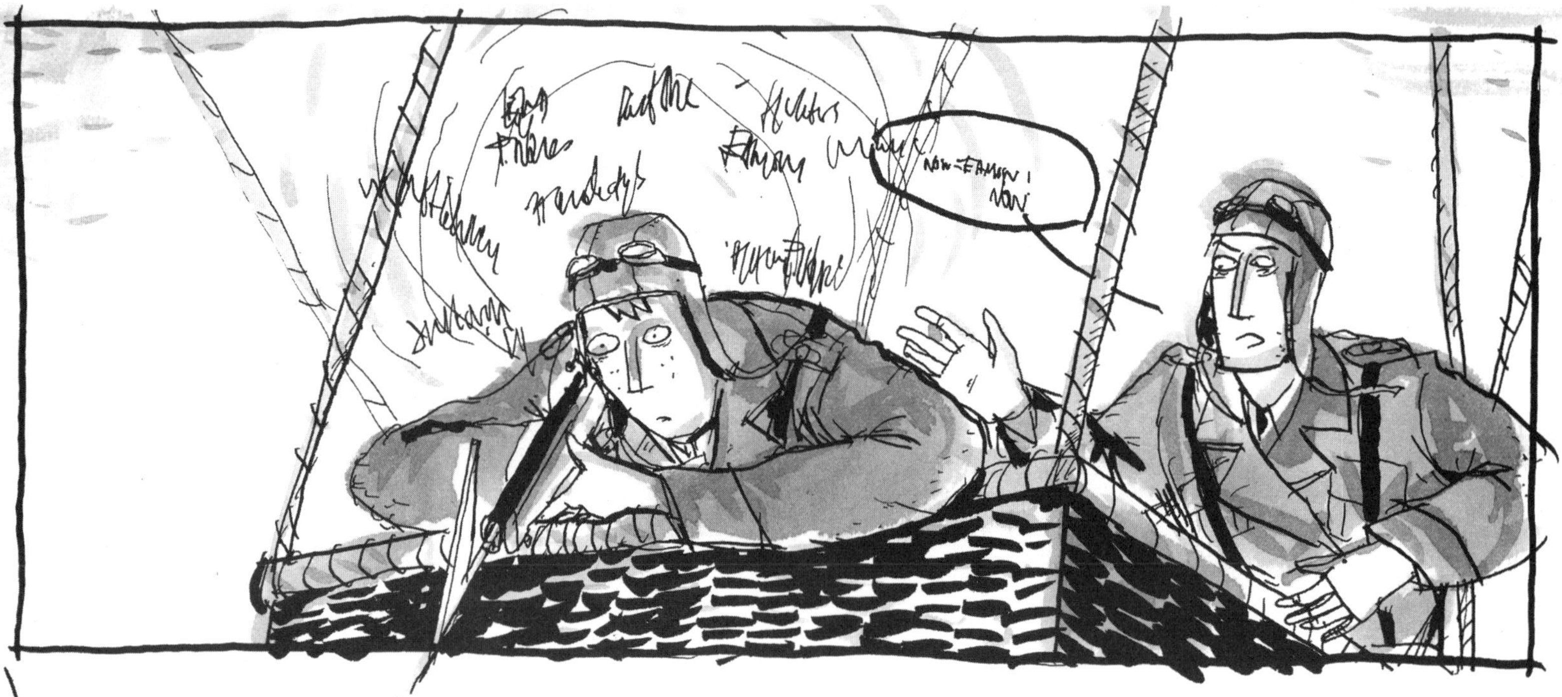
NOW—EAMON! NOW!

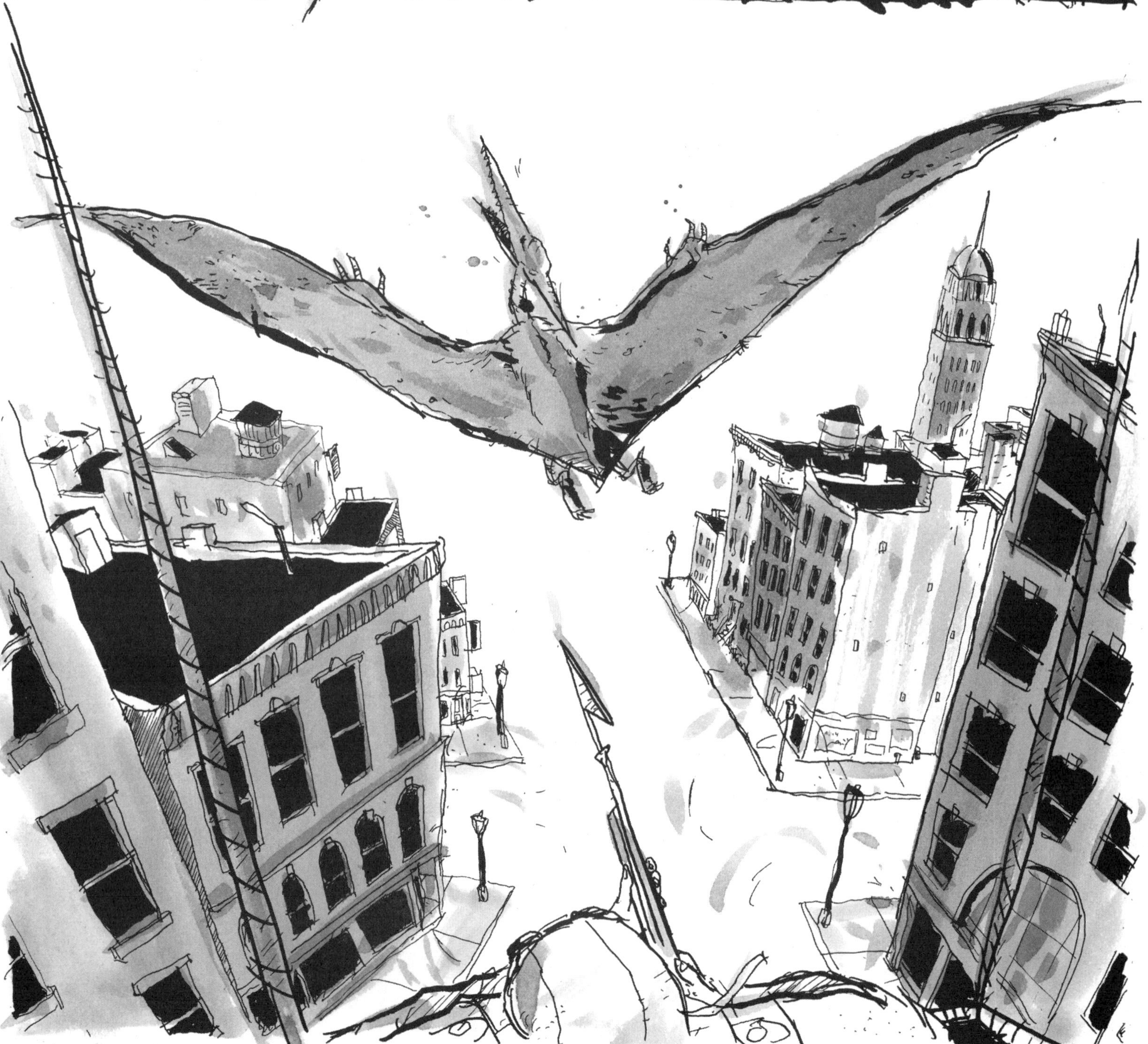

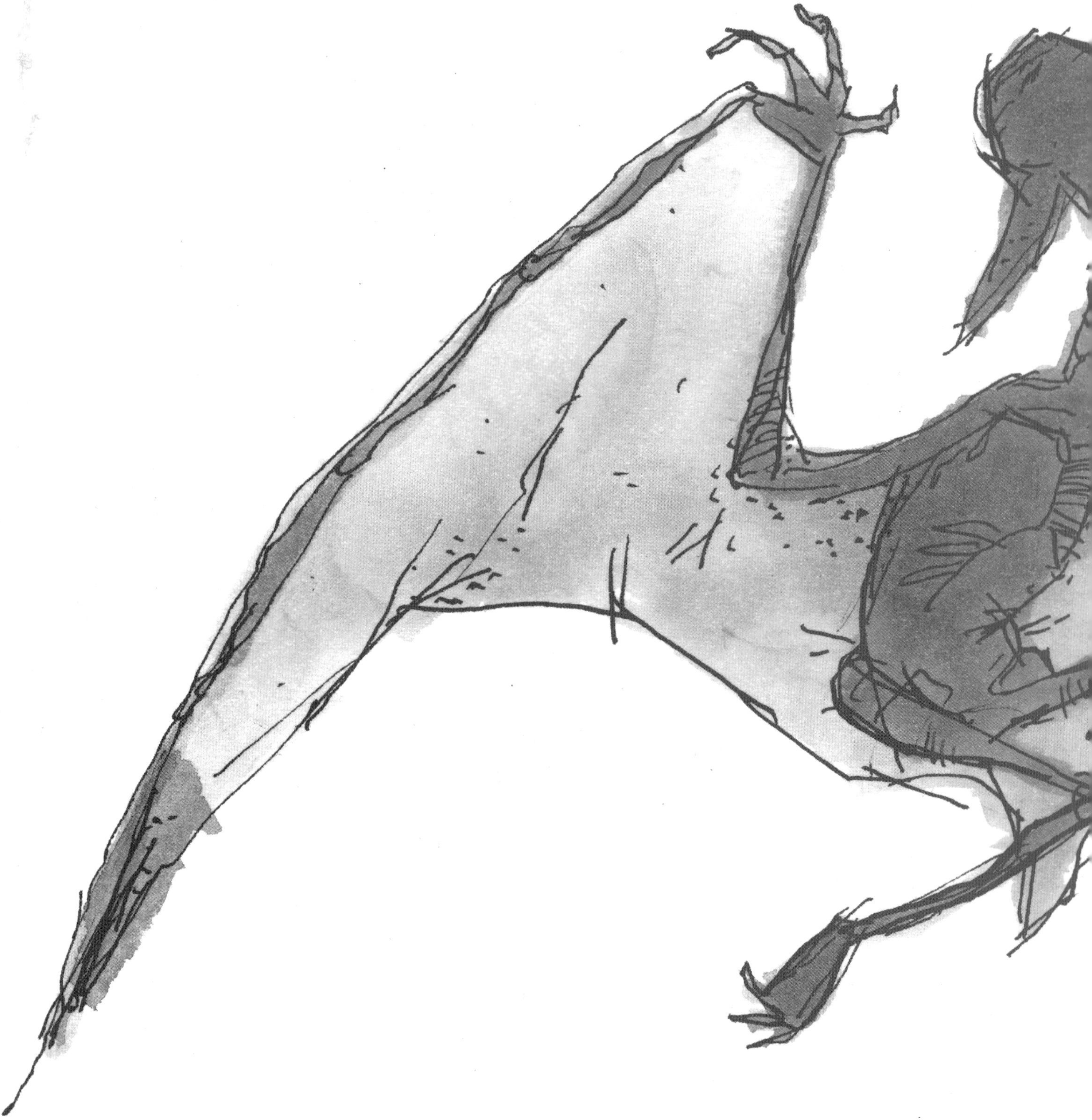

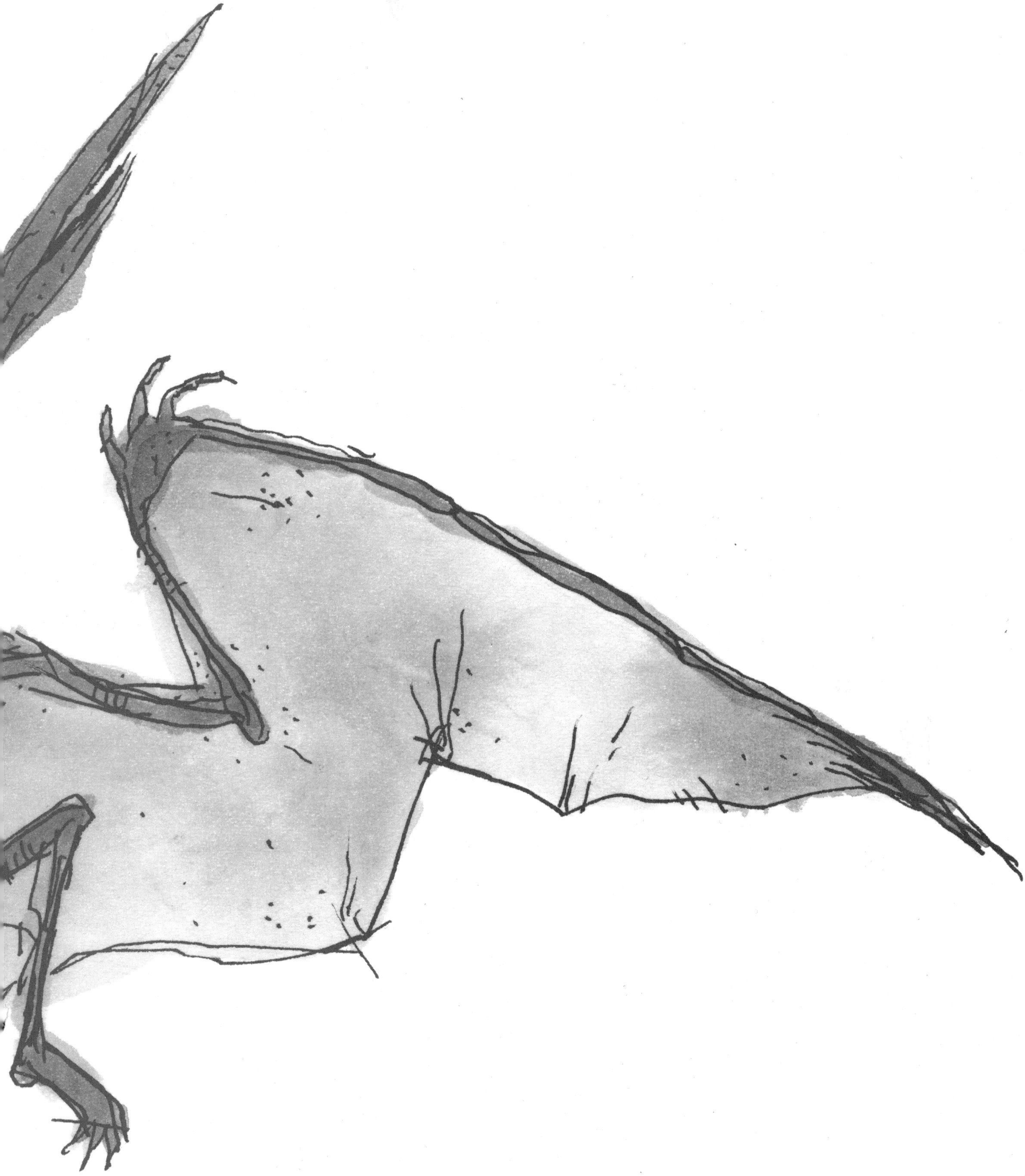

TRUSTEES CONFIRM RENO AS CITY MARSHAL

The board met in regular session Tuesday evening at 7:30 o'clock p. m. President R. B. Haydock and Trustees Spence, Coen Holst and Parish present. The minutes of the previous meeting were read and approved.

On motion of Spence, seconded by Parish, President R. B. Haydock was appointed to attend the convention, at Los Angeles on January 30th, to consider the construction of a highway along the line of the Camino Real.

The clerk was ordered to have the surveyor set grade stake so property owners could pave on front of their property.

The following claims were ordered paid:

Colonia Improv. Co., water   826.66
Electric Lights   8.35

The board approved the official bond of W. C. Reno as marshal and ex-officio tax and license collector.

Board adjourned.

EXTRA PEACE OFFICERS BRING SUIT

Ventura Democrat: Eugene Fordyce, who has been acting as constable of Ventura Township, by virtue of a certificate of election issued to him by the Board of Supervisors, but whose bills for services were rejected, has filed an action against the county to recover the sum of 81,309.90, being the aggregate sum of his claim and those of Wesley Boling, Fred Lynn and J. P. Mehn—the latter gentlemen having assigned their claims to Mr. Fordyce. The complaint alleges that he received the highest number of votes cast for constable in Ventura Township and that a certification of election was issued him. That from January to July he performed the service of such office, and duly filed his claim, which was rejected. The claims are: Fordyce, 8391.80; Boling, 8381; Lynn, 8318.10; Mehn, 8219.

REBEKAHS GIVE ENJOYABLE PARTY

The ladies of the Fleur-de-lis Rebekahs Lodge gave a surprise party Wednesday evening at the home of Dr. and Mrs. Dumont Dwire, as a farewell to Mr. and Mrs. Homer Coffee, who depart Friday for Los Angeles.

The evening was spent with games and music. Light refreshments were served.

Those present were: Messrs and Mesdames Dumont Dwire, Homer Coffee, F. W. Train, B. F. Meyers, Chas. Peile, Chas. F. Ruggles, Roy Huffman, Hugh Thatcher, M. J. Ely, and W. B. Cooper.

Mrs. Kate Newby.

Misses Louise Burgess and Marian Bither.

A PRISONER IN HER OWN HOUSE.

Mrs. W. H. Layha, of 1001 Agnes Ave., Kansas City, Mo., has for several years been troubled with severe hoarseness and at times a hard cough, which she says "Would keep me in doors for days. I was prescribed for by physicians with no

ABOUT LEFT MINDED PEOPLE

Both sides of the brain are capable of performing the duties of giving commands to the limbs, but the orders only come from one side, either from the right or left, but if the side upon which the speech center lies gets injured and is rendered incapable of performing its duty then the other side takes up the work, though it requires some time before it can do so properly.

Supposing a man meets with a bad fall or accident of any kind which damages the speech center on the left, he becomes dumb for the time being. Then the right side slowly learns how to give orders, and the man gradually regains power of speech after some years, but in many cases he becomes left handed because now the orders from the brain are transmitted more rapidly to the left than to the right.

You have often experienced, I suppose, the curious feeling that you have done something or met some one at some time or other when in reality you have not done so at all.

Supposing the left side of your brain conceived the idea that you were going to tie your boot lace and that the right side was, say, a thousandth part of a second behindhand in grasping the same idea, the result, when the right side did grasp it, would be that you would imagine that you had already tied your boot lace.—Dr. Withrow in London Answers.

Dreams of Peace Allure to Death.

Dreams of peace have always allured mankind to their undoing. Human destiny has been wrought out through war. The United States is an illustration. Little of the soil which now acknowledges the sovereignty of the Union has not been subdued by arms. The first settlers slew the Indians or were themselves slain; next the Americans and English conquered the French; afterward the Americans turned on the English and, with the aid of France, ejected them. In 1812 we again fought the English to defend the national unity and subsequently took California from Mexico by the sword. To consolidate a homogeneous empire we crushed the social system of the south, and lastly we cast forth Spain. The story is written in blood, and common sense teaches us that as the past has been, so will be the future. Nature has decreed that animals shall compete for life, or, in other words, destroy or be destroyed. We can hope for no exemption from the common lot.—Brook Adams in Atlantic.

London's Whistles.

A boy was charged at a London police court the other day with blowing a whistle in such a way as to cause three policemen to come toward him. The fact that such a thing is possible suggests the questions: How do the police distinguish between a cab whistle and a police whistle? What is there to prevent any one from blowing a whistle in such a way as to call a policeman?

A representative of the Graphic who put these questions to a high official of the city police learned that in the matter of attending to whistles, as with his many other duties, the policeman uses his discretion. Any shrill whistle will attract a policeman, but such a whistle blown at night outside a restaurant or any place where people congregate and cabs are wanted would not bring a policeman to the whistler. The same whistle blown in precisely the same way in the middle of the city at midday would bring a policeman on the scene at once.—London Graphic.

Lakes of Blood.

The name Lake of Blood or its equivalent has been given to places as far apart as England and South America. "Sanguelac"—i. e. the Lake of Blood—was the name given by the victorious Normans to the battlefield at Hast-

RUGGLES RECEIVES A NEW CONDENSER FOR WATER

C. F. Ruggles has received a brand new condenser from the east and is now in splendid shape to furnish the best possible distilled water. He has sent a sample to Prof. Hilgard at the University of California to have analyzed. Mr. Ruggles guarantees his distilled water to be as good as the best, and he desires the people of Oxnard to try his house manufacture.

WORKING NIGHT AND DAY.

The busiest and mightiest little thing that ever was made is Dr. King's New Life Pills. These pills change weakness into strength, listlessness into energy, brain-fag into mental power. They're wonderful in building up the health. Only 25c per box. Sold by Ben S. Virden.

Pumping plants a specialty at Pettis & Brenneis. Jackson pumps, Fairbanks and Lambert engines. 3-tf

LINERS.

WANTED TO RENT—A nice house in good neighborhood. Apply at this office.   3tf

FOR RENT—Part of store room, suitable for music, jewelry or books and stationery. Enquire at Oxnard Courier office.

FOR SALE—Stove wood.
Kindling wood.
One off leader, weight about 1450 lbs.
One single buggy horse—cheap.
One wagon and beet bed.
One wagon.
Two disc plows 3 gang, used one season.
One Stallion "Sid" by Siddartha.
Three walking plows.
One water tank.
Two beet cultivators.
Two beet plows.
Enquire of E.R. Hill, Oxnard, Cal.

STOVE WOOD—87 a cord delivered. See J. J. Moraga at El Rio or leave orders at F. L. Holmes, liquorhouse, Oxnard.   52tf

TWO FINE KENTUCKY JACKS—Will make the season commencing January 1, 1904 at Lee Richardson's place, one mile north of Oxnard. Terms: 820 to insure fold, 815 for the season. C. F Beckwith & Lewis owners; L. Bilbartz, keeper. 50-6mo

RESIDENCE LOTS FOR SALE—two east front corner lots in the most desirable part of town. Apply to H. L. Wineman, Wineman Co. Oxnard   50tf

FOR SALE—Pure olive oil put up in bottles and cans. Wholesale or retail. Address N. W. Crain, Simi, Cal.   44tf

FOR SALE—Fine apples, cheap, on trees, or delivered. N. W. Crain, Simi, Cal.   44-tf

FOR SALE or Rent—At a bargain equity in 4 room house and lot, including good furniture in choice neighborhood, $200.00 cash. Address Oxnard. Lock Box 48.   tf

FOR SALE—Horse, buggy and harness For price and terms enquire Ben S. Virden.

A Bald Statement